P H

Christine Pullein-Thompson has lived with horses all her life. At the age of four she fell off the elephant at the London Zoo and by the age of twelve had fallen off ponies more than a hundred times! When she was nearly fifteen, she and her sisters, Josephine and twin Diana, started a riding school, which grew until at one time they had more than forty horses in their stables. They trained and mounted the first team to win the Pony Club Inter-Branch Competition and also became honorary whippers-in to the Woodland Foxhounds.

Christine is well-known as the author of many novels about ponies and horses, and wrote her first book, *We Rode to the Sea*, in her teens. Since then she has had nearly fifty books published.

She is married to a BBC Monitor, also an author, and they live in Oxfordshire with their four children, three horses, a dog, two cats and a tame hen.

This Armada book belongs to:

Other titles by Christine Pullein-Thompson in Armada

Goodbye to Hounds
Stolen Ponies
I Rode a Winner
The Horse Sale
Ride by Night

in the same series

Phantom Horse Comes Home
Phantom Horse Goes to Ireland
Phantom Horse in Danger

also

Good Riding
Riding For Fun
Improve Your Riding

First published in the U.K. in 1955 by
Wm. Collins Sons & Co. Ltd., London and Glasgow.
This edition was first published in Armada in 1969 by
Fontana Paperbacks,
14 St. James's Place, London SW1A 1PS

This impression 1980

© Christine Pullein-Thompson 1955

Printed in Great Britain by
Love & Malcomson Ltd., Brighton Road,
Redhill, Surrey, England.

CONDITIONS OF SALE:
This book is sold subject to the condition
that it shall not, by way of trade or otherwise,
be lent, re-sold, hired out or otherwise circulated
without the publisher's prior consent in any form of
binding or cover other than that in which it is
published and without a similar condition
including this condition being imposed
on the subsequent purchaser.

PHANTOM HORSE

CHRISTINE PULLEIN-THOMPSON

Armada

ILLUSTRATIONS

CHAPTER ONE

"WE'VE GOT news for you," Daddy said, brandishing a letter.

I thought, a new pony, and saw a gay, grey four-year-old grazing with Moonlight and Mermaid in the paddock. My brother Angus was looking out of the window to where the lawn was dappled with sunlight.

"We're all going to Washington," Daddy said.

For an awful moment I couldn't think where in the world Washington was situated. Then Angus enlightened me.

"You mean America?" he asked incredulously.

"Yes, to the United States of America for three years," Daddy replied.

I felt a lump rising in my throat. I didn't want to live in America. And what was to happen to Moonlight and Mermaid? And what would we do with Sparrow Cottage?

Angus was more sensible. "What fun!" he exclaimed gaily. "But what will we do with the ponies? We can't take them, can we?"

"You can lend them to anyone you like," Mummy replied. "We'll let the cottage, and you'll go to American schools."

"We'll be living outside Washington, so you'll be able to ride as long as it isn't too expensive," Daddy said in reassuring accents.

"Lots of Americans ride, particularly in Virginia. I think you'll have a lovely time," Mummy told us.

"Will we go by ship or air?" Angus asked. "How long will it take to get there?" He sounded excited. I imagined him telling the boys at his school all about it.

5

"By sea. It'll take anything from four to eight days depending on which boat we catch," Daddy replied.

"Oh, I hope we go on one of the *Queens* or on the *United States*," Angus cried.

I think I had better explain that Daddy is in the Foreign Service and liable to be sent anywhere at any time. It might have been Cairo, or Paris, or Pakistan, or Chile or Australia. Really it was lucky for us that we were to go to America, for at least we could all go, and there would be suitable schools, and we more or less knew the language. I thought of all this as I looked at our ponies grazing in the paddock beneath the tall elms, which are supposed to be dangerous, but at this moment were just turning green and looked wizard against the shifting April sky.

We discussed America for ages and all the time I had an empty feeling in the pit of my stomach. Angus seemed terribly excited. He has Daddy's mania for travel; they're really very alike, both having dark hair, brown eyes and rather sensitive faces.

I'm more like Mummy, who has nut-brown hair and blue eyes. I could see that she didn't want to move either, as we all stood together in the little front room we called the nursery, on that sparkling April day.

I thought of all we would be leaving behind—friends, ponies, early morning rides through sombre beech woods, hunting, gymkhanas, the Pony Club, Sparrow Cottage. I didn't think America would give us much in exchange for these. Little did I dream then of the crises and adventures which awaited us in Virginia, or that one day I should come to love the Blue Ridge Mountains, almost as much as I loved Oxfordshire.

America held all our thoughts for the rest of the holidays. We were to leave on July 30th. Angus stayed madly gay. He rushed about the house singing from dawn to dusk, and talked ceaselessly about the voyage and the colossal size of New York. He seemed to have collected a great deal of information in a very short time.

We loaned Moonlight and Mermaid to a nearby family who had never been rich enough to buy ponies of their own. We tidied up the house and decided what we would take and what we would leave behind; and, since we were leaving England straight from school, we said good-bye to all our local friends.

Saying good-bye was really the worst part of all. Three years seems such a long time when the moment comes to bid farewell to people you have known all your life. For the first time I was glad when the holidays were over.

But school wasn't much better. My friends all seemed envious of my trip to the United States. They couldn't leave the subject alone. "You'll come back very grown-up with a petal cut and lots of lipstick," they told me.

"And you'll think of nothing but boys," Pat Clayton added. "And dress like a bobby soxer," June said.

"It'll be wizard!" cried Pat wistfully. "Think of seeing the Empire State Building and the White House! You don't seem a bit excited. Honestly, you are queer."

I couldn't explain how I hated leaving Sparrow Cottage and the ponies, or that I didn't think anything could be as beautiful as the beech woods of Oxfordshire with the sun shining through the trees; or the orchards in the early morning half-hidden in an autumn mist.

"You've jolly well got to write to us anyway—lots and lots of postcards," Pam said.

"And try to send as many different stamps as you can," June told me.

"I'll do my best," I promised.

Fortunately term passed very quickly. Mummy wrote to say that we were to live in a small, white house in the heart of Virginia. "And you'll be lent ponies and there's a paddock and what Americans call a barn," she added in a postscript, and I suddenly felt much happier. I imagined a paddock with elm trees and a kind of Dutch barn.

The last day of term arrived followed by the traditional midnight feasts. I ate vast quantities of cake, and hot dogs smuggled from Marks and Spencers in my honour, and chocolate and gob stoppers.

Pam, June and Pat drank my health in fizzy lemonade and wished me luck in the States. And I suddenly began to feel quite sad. I knew that none of us would be the same in three years time. I might not even return to the same school.

"I really will write," I said now. "And you must write too, because I shall want to know how you all are. And who's left, and whether old Bumble's just the same."

Bumble was our nickname for the headmistress. Her real name was Florence Bee, but to the school she was Bumble and had been, I suspect, for years.

June began to laugh then and we all felt much better. "That old war-horse will never change," she said.

We started singing after that; and eventually retired to bed at about two in the morning, after running round the garden in our pyjamas.

July 30th dawned fair. I said good-bye to everyone, and Bumble said that she hoped I would always remember the old school, and cherish my years there as some of the happiest of my life. Everyone else wished me good luck, and silly things like lots to eat, and prosperous days. I was glad when eventually Mummy, Daddy and Angus arrived in the car and I waved my last good-byes, and we drove down the short wooded drive for the last time.

We spent the night in a simply huge hotel in London. Our bedrooms had automatic locks and Angus locked himself out of his five times. I lost my key twice and locked myself out of mine three times. Luckily the Cockney chambermaids were very good-tempered, and rocked with laughter whenever they saw us and rushed for skeleton keys. All the same we felt the most terrible country bumpkins.

It was raining when we sailed from Southampton, which somehow seemed appropriate. I remember that we were all rather gloomy and a little sentimental about leaving England.

8

We went out by tug to a Dutch ship which had come from Holland and France. There was a heavy mist. It might have been October rather than July.

Since this book is mainly concerned with Angus's and my adventures in America, I'm not going to tell you much about the voyage, though we all enjoyed it enormously. There was masses to eat, and dancing sometimes in the evenings, and a game called Bingo. And there were turtle races which I didn't enjoy because I was sorry for the turtles. Although it was quite a small ship, there was a library and film shows and draught and chess boards and, of course, packs of cards. There was deck tennis and a peculiar deck game with squares which Angus and I never really mastered. There was a tiny swimming-pool and a gym, but the weather was cloudy and cold, so the pool was never filled, and only the few Americans on board used the gym. There were several bars and a palm court lounge.

I had the upper berth in the cabin I shared with Mummy, which meant I climbed to bed by ladder. Mummy and I were sick for the whole of one day. We all went to Church on Sunday, at least it wasn't really Church but a service conducted by the Captain which lasted for hours. As it was in Dutch we couldn't understand one word and Angus fell asleep with his mouth open.

The next day we saw the skyscrapers of New York for the first time. The weather had improved and the sun was shining. For us it was a historic occasion, and I must say New York did look lovely. It was the first time we had seen land since the Isle of Wight and all but the hardened travellers on board were tremendously excited. We crowded the upper decks and some Americans started to sing *America* and an old lady burst into tears.

Soon we could see the Statue of Liberty and a vast harbour full of ships. A few minutes later the immigration authorities arrived by tug and with them the *New York Times*. The ship's loudspeaker started calling people to the dining-room and giving information about visas and passports and currency. There was a great deal of bustle and everywhere people were saying good-bye to friends they had made on board and might never see again. The American travellers were soon finished with the necessary formalities, but the rest of us had to have visas stamped, and questions asked about why we had come to America and where we were going and how long we were staying. Mummy was rather cross and said that America didn't seem like a free country any more.

And then at last we were docked in Hoboken and Angus and I stepped on American soil for the first time. The customs were marvellously organised and in a matter of minutes we were bowling through New York in a taxi towards Pennsylvania railway station.

Angus was rather overcome by everything. He kept saying, "It's supersonic! Isn't it? Absolutely supersonic." He said it quite indiscriminately as we travelled through New York. I think he was still seeing the beautiful harbour, and the skyscrapers looking like a vast pile of immense boxes against the blue sky.

We passed two police horses and Times Square, which is rather like Piccadilly, but even worse. Angus was surprised to see trams, or what Americans call street cars. I had expected New York to look much cleaner. We saw the Lever Brothers building, which is enormously tall and built of glass, so that you can see everyone working inside.

Pennsylvania railway station seemed enormous. There were thousands of people and loudspeakers talking continuously. We had time for a few sandwiches at a huge soda fountain and then it was time to board the train for Washington.

The train wasn't like an English train. Down each side there were pairs of seats, which would tip back or turn round, about twenty or thirty to a carriage. There was a bar on the train, where people were playing cards, and a dining-car. At intervals a negro passed along the corridor between the seats offering things like chocolate and cigarettes, coffee, Coca-Cola, sandwiches. There was a drinking fountain at the end of each carriage, with cardboard beakers, where you could help yourself.

The train journey passed very quickly. In what seemed no time at all, we came to Washington. Our luggage had travelled from New York in the baggage car; now a negro porter collected it for us from the baggage room. Mummy was rather overcome when she found that the porter charged twenty-five cents for each piece of luggage, which since there were eight pieces, meant we had to tip him two dollars, roughly fourteen shillings.

We sat outside the station looking at the special traffic lights provided for pedestrians, while Daddy found the car allotted to him during our stay in America.

We felt very gay as we drove out of Washington on the last lap of our long journey.

The Capitol looked wonderful against the blue sky, white and clear cut and terribly impressive. The car seemed enormous; Daddy drove very slowly, pointing out places of interest. I'm afraid I was too excited to take much in. I was far more interested in seeing our new home and the ponies we were to ride than places of historic interest. I missed the White House altogether and hardly noticed the Potomac river gleaming in the sunlight. The road from Washington was broad and straight and for the first time I realised why Americans like fast cars.

"We're in Virginia now," Daddy told us.

And then, at last, we saw our house. It stood on the side of a hill and was white, and built mostly of wood. It was called simply Mountain Farm, and I think I loved it from the first moment. Behind the house there was a building, which looked like a stable, and then a field fenced by walls. After that the land was rough and strewn with boulders, until it reached the Blue Ridge Mountains, which aren't really mountains in the European sense, but more like wild, wooded hills.

We approached Mountain Farm by what Americans

11

call a dirt road. As we drew near, I saw that a stream ran along one side of the house, and that there was a small lawn in front and some trees.

"Well, do you like it?" Daddy asked.

Angus and I were very enthusiastic. Mummy said:

"Don't be too pleased. We haven't seen inside yet."

"And the stables may be awful," Daddy added.

There was a hammock slung between the trees on the lawn, and a garage at the back of the house.

"The ponies haven't come yet," Daddy said, after we had put the car away. "The paddock's completely empty. I'll ring up Charlie to-night—just to let him know we're here."

Charlie Miller is an old school friend of Daddy's, who married a rich American and has lived in Virginia ever since. It was he who found us Mountain Farm and promised to lend us ponies.

The house was sweet inside, with a large kitchen, a tiny dining-room, a sitting-room and three bedrooms. There was also a bathroom, and a larder which we found already stocked with food. There was a huge piece of smoked ham hanging from a hook, a heap of American corn, a whole shelf of tinned goods, a can of milk, cheese, eggs and butter, and some obviously home-made bread.

It was Angus's and my first taste of American generosity and we were rather surprised.

"That's just like Charlie and Ann," Daddy said.

"They must be jolly nice people," Angus replied. "Do you think all this stuff is really a present?"

"I suspect so," Daddy answered.

Mummy and I started to prepare a hasty meal, while Daddy and Angus carried the luggage upstairs. We found that we had been provided with an electric cooker, a washing-up machine, a refrigerator and a washing machine. Mummy and I cooked ham and eggs, to be followed by bread and cheese. We all felt rather sleepy, but very gay when we sat down to supper. It was nearly dark outside and the mountains looked blue and misty and romantic. Fresh air floated into the kitchen smelling a little like mountain air and, at the same time, of dry earth, boxwood and burnt grass.

When we had washed up—in the sink, because none of us felt enterprising enough to brave the washing-up machine—we wandered outside to admire the landscape. It was then that we heard the sound of a car coming along the dirt road and saw the flash of headlights.

"Not visitors already?" Mummy exclaimed.

"It's probably Charlie. He never could wait for anything," Daddy replied.

The car swung into our yard, and, for a moment, we were all blinded by its lights. Then a chorus of voices cried, "Hiya," and suddenly the yard was full of people. Daddy was shaking someone warmly by the hand and introducing us all to Mr. and Mrs. Miller, who introduced their three children, Phil, Pete and Wendy. I felt in a daze and suddenly shy. The Miller children looked so old, years older than Angus and me. Wendy took charge of us. She explained that she and her brothers lived just over the hill. She asked whether the food had arrived all right and whether we liked Mountain Farm. She wanted to know whether we had enjoyed our trip and how long it had taken. Then Phil interrupted. "We'll be bringing a couple of horses over for you to-morrow," he said.

Before we could say thank you, Pete said, "Has anyone told them about the wild horse?"

"No, tell them, Wendy," Phil answered.

"There's a wild horse around here in the mountains," Wendy began, and I saw by the light of the headlights that she had hazel eyes and was nearly as tall as Pete, but that neither she nor Peter were as tall as Phil, who towered above us all.

"At least he's not really wild," she continued. "He's a full bred horse with a touch of Arab in him, but he is really a Palomino because of his colour. He's the most beautiful horse you've ever seen, and whoever catches him can have him, that's the deal."

I suddenly didn't feel sleepy any more. If only Angus and I could catch him . . . I thought. If only . . .

"They wanted to try him on the race track," Pete said. "I guess he's the fastest little horse in the state of Virginia. We want you two to help us catch him. Then we can tame him together."

Charlie Miller interrupted. "Don't you listen to them, son," he said, slapping Angus on the back. "No one will ever catch that darned horse. He's as wild as they're made and nuts into the bargain. One day someone will get up and shoot him and get a few dollars for his hide."

"Boy! You should see him jump," Wendy exclaimed, ignoring her father. "All the mares are crazy about him. They jump out of their fields and disappear, sometimes for weeks on end. That's why everyone's so mad about him."

"And remember whoever catches him keeps him," Pete said.

"We'd love to help you," I said. "We've ridden quite a bit, though we aren't experts by any means."

"We'd sure appreciate your help," Phil replied. "With five of us we might drive him into a corral."

"Come on home," said Mr. Miller. "That's enough of that darned horse for one night."

Phil, Pete and Wendy shook us by the hand before they left, and I noticed that they were all wearing jeans and checked shirts, and canvas shoes which we later learned to call sneakers.

The yard was very quiet when the Millers had gone.

Mummy said, "What an invasion. But it was nice of them to call."

None of us could keep our eyes open any longer. Mummy leaned wearily against the garage wall.

"I suppose we ought to have asked them in," she said. "We weren't very hospitable."

"I did, but they didn't want to bother us," Daddy replied.

"Isn't it wonderful about the horse?" Angus asked.

14

"Just supposing Jean and I caught him. We'd really have a horse of our own then."

I felt too tired to speak. A century seemed to have passed since we left England.

"I don't want you to do anything reckless," Mummy said, moving towards the house.

"Remember, this isn't England, and it's easy to get lost," Daddy warned us. "Charlie's children are very anxious to ride with you and I don't want you to ride alone, for the time being anyway. Is that quite clear?"

"Quite," I replied.

"We'll remember," Angus promised.

"How about bed?" Mummy suggested.

My bedroom was at the back of the house. It looked across the field to the mountains. It smelt of washed linen and boxwood. There was the painting of a horse above my bed and a pile of books on a table. The walls were white and newly painted. There were rush mats on the floor. I turned the books over and saw that they were without exception about horses, and that in each Wendy's name was clearly written on the flyleaf. So she had left them here for me I realised and I marvelled again at the Millers' hospitality and generosity. Had Peter and Phil left books for Angus? I wondered.

The last thing I saw before I fell asleep was a large orange moon riding high over the mountains.

CHAPTER TWO

I WAKENED next morning with a light heart. Birds were singing outside my window. The sky was a cloudless blue. So this is America, I thought dreamily, climbing from my comfortable bed to gaze at the Blue Mountains, serene and beautiful in the sunlight. It was still early but already there were coloured men hurrying across the

15

hill to the farm below. I could hear some of them singing; and from the highway came the distant sound of cars.

A girl in jeans stepped out of a van and put letters in our box by the gate. She was singing a sloppy sort of love song; she was small and active with long fair hair.

Later the Millers arrived with a clatter of hoofs which fetched us all from the kitchen where we were eating

Coming into the yard with the sun behind them

breakfast. They looked marvellous coming into the yard with the sun behind them, like something out of a Wild West film. They were mounted on a variety of horses: Phil rode a tall, dun mare with a fiddle face and large ears; Wendy was on a roan pony of about thirteen hands; Pete sat astride a chestnut with a streak of white down her face.

"Hi. Are we too early for you?" Wendy cried as we

emerged. "We thought you wouldn't want to wait to see your horses."

Angus was still half asleep. Five minutes ago he had been in bed fast asleep.

"It's jolly nice of you to bring them," I replied, looking at the horses Pete and Phil were leading. One was a nicely marked skewbald, the other a bay.

"I hope they're all right," Wendy said anxiously. She looked even larger, sitting astride the little roan, than she had in the dusk the evening before. She was wearing a red checked shirt and the inevitable jeans; her hair appeared almost chestnut in the sunshine.

"They look absolutely super," I replied, patting the skewbald's neck.

"What does super mean?" Peter asked. Angus started to explain.

"They're nothing of the kind," Phil said after a moment. "The spotted mare's lazy and the bay mare's just a green four-year-old. But maybe you'll make something of them. They've been reared on the mountains or near enough, and that's important, because it means they know their way around. An imported horse doesn't last a month over here."

"Well, thanks very much for lending them to us," I replied.

"Yes, thanks," said Angus.

"I shouldn't say too much until you've ridden them," Phil answered and I saw that he was laughing.

The Millers were riding on a variety of saddles. Wendy had a steeplechase saddle on her roan and rode with short stirrups. Phil was riding long with a Western saddle and wooden stirrups. Peter looked cramped on a straight-cut show saddle, which appeared out of place with the breast-plate and martingale he had attached.

Wendy's eyes followed mine. She said, "We've lent you a couple of English Whippy saddles. I hope you like them".

"They're super. Much better than anything we've got at home," Angus answered.

"It's jolly nice of you to lend us so much," I said, looking at the horses' shoes which had calkins both hind and fore.

"We came early because in a couple of hours it will be too hot to ride," Peter told us.

"Okay, we'll dash and change. Come on, Angus," I cried, remembering that I was dressed only in shorts and a sort of sun top.

"We won't be a sec'," Angus cried, before following in my wake.

"They look quite different on horses. Bigger but not so terrifying," Angus said, as we hurried into the kitchen.

"You can't be frightened of them. You're not, are you?" I asked. "They seem absolutely harmless to me—just terribly generous."

"No, I'm not a bit. I just think they look a bit tough. Did you notice that Wendy was chewing gum?" Angus replied.

"That doesn't mean a person's tough," I answered, looking round the kitchen.

Our parents were on the lawn examining the peach tree.

"Don't you think we'd better do something about the breakfast things before we leave?" Angus asked. "It won't take a minute with all these machines."

I could see that he was longing to try the washing-up machine. I thought of the Millers waiting outside.

"We'll have to be terribly quick," I replied, madly collecting plates.

When the machine was full we put soap powder through a hole in the top and turned it on.

"They'll be washed by the time we've changed," Angus said cheerfully, giving the machine an admiring glance.

We put on jodhpurs and aertex shirts, and I dragged a comb through my hair and wished that my eyes were

18

hazel like Wendy's instead of large and blue—doll's eyes Angus called them.

We tore down to the kitchen together and found the floor flooded. Angus gave a cry of anguish. "It's sicked up everything. Oh, the beast!" he cried.

The wretched machine was smugly purring.

"I'm sure we didn't do anything wrong," I said, looking at the pool of water on the floor. "It's just beastly, that's all."

Angus seized a mop and the handle immediately fell off, then I ran into him when I was looking frantically for a floor cloth. We were like a couple of tiresome clowns without being funny, and we started to get furious with one another.

"Why can't you look where you're going?" cried Angus.

"None of this would have happened if you hadn't wanted to use that silly machine," I retorted.

Angus found some sort of cloth at last and started to mop the floor.

"Well, I'm not going to risk it again anyway," I said, taking the crockery out of the machine and putting it in the sink.

"The Millers must be sick and tired of waiting. We're really treating them very badly," Angus said.

"Well, they might have guessed we couldn't manage machines," I replied crossly.

At last the breakfast things were washed and we dashed outside. The Millers were calmly talking to Daddy and I realised that our rushing and panic had been quite unnecessary. They looked as though they could wait all day quite happily chatting in the sunshine.

"The spotted mare's for you. Her name's Frances," Phil told me. He held her head while I mounted and helped me adjust my stirrups. It felt marvellous to be on a horse again.

Frances was narrow with a prominent wither and rather long ears. Her mane changed colour half-way up her neck and three of her hoofs were light coloured. She felt tall

19

after Moonlight and Mermaid who are only fourteen hands.

Angus mounted the bay. She had a well-cut, keen head and an excitable eye. She stood about fifteen one and Angus's feet only reached six inches below the saddle flaps.

Mummy appeared from the house and said, "Why haven't you put these on?" and waved our crash caps. We had always worn them at home, but seeing the Millers dressed so casually had made us leave them where they were in our bedrooms. Now we felt foolish.

"This isn't our lucky day. First the washing machine, then the hats," Angus muttered.

"You are mutts," Mummy said. "Why do you think you're less likely to have accidents here than at home?"

"It wasn't that," I replied.

"What was it then?" she asked, and we felt more foolish than ever.

"Oh nothing," Angus said.

"Do you always wear hats then?" Wendy asked.

I thought, hats, hats, hats. Will they never stop talking about hats?

"More or less. Mummy likes us to anyway," Angus replied. We put on our hats.

"We wear them hunting of course," Wendy told us.

"Mind you're back by one," Daddy said.

"Be careful," Mummy added.

We rode out of the yard into the bright sunshine. Frances jogged. Angus grinned and said, "Our first ride in Virginia, Jean."

I felt like singing. America seemed far nicer than I had ever thought possible. I imagined the letters I would write home to Pam and Pat and June. I was certain that Angus and I were destined to be happy at Mountain Farm.

There was an odd humming noise in the air rather like the incessant buzz of flies but with more of a croak in it and more substance. As we rode along the dirt road, Phil said:

"If you're trying to guess what the peculiar noise is, Jean, I'll tell you—it's the frogs. The land around here is full of them. Sometimes you can hear them the whole night long."

I imagined thousands of frogs. "Gosh, I never knew there was so much wild life in America. I knew there were ranches and cowboys, but I thought the rest of it was all very new and modern."

The Millers laughed.

"Not Virginia, it's tough," Pete replied, laughing at me with his grey eyes. "Why, there're wild cats and bears in the mountains."

"And deer and grey foxes," Wendy added.

"Not forgetting the wild horse we hope to show you to-day," Phil said.

Frances was quiet with a long easy stride. Her long ears flopped backwards and forwards as she walked. Coloured women were picking blackberries from a wayside bush.

"They make them into wine," Peter told us. "They get quite drunk on it sometimes."

"Do you mind jumping a wall?" Wendy asked.

"Not a bit," I replied.

"I'd love to," Angus said.

I just had time to grab France's mane before we were cantering towards the three-foot wall which ran along one side of the dirt road. Frances took off rather late and I lost both stirrups and ended up by her ears. The bay mare refused, but jumped it when Angus tried again.

We cantered on across marshy land intersected by little streams. Here the frogs' singing was much louder and at intervals I saw their heads sticking out through the grass. There were Hereford cattle grazing in the fields, and in the distance we could see tractors and horses carting corn. Frances was going beautifully, and I felt like singing as we left the flat land behind, jumped some rails in single file, and cantered up a gentle sloping hill. I think Angus was finding the bay mare rather strong.

He was crouched over her withers, and each time she snatched at the reins, he seemed to tip a little farther forward.

When we reached the edge of the mountains, the Millers halted their horses and turned them round.

"See down there, there's your house," Phil told us, pointing.

The valley lay before us parched and sunlit. There were cattle and stone walls, white houses, shabby wooden shacks and farms, and, farther away, the long straight line of the highway. Our own house looked very small standing alone at the end of the dirt road.

"Nice view, huh?" inquired Wendy.

"You wait until we reach the view pole. Then you'll really be seeing something," Phil said.

And now we turned again and followed a trail. At first it was wide and grassy with trees on each side; but gradually it narrowed and there were boulders, and it twisted and turned, and low branches scraped our heads. The going became steadily worse and, at one time, we seemed to be riding up the bed of a stream, and twice we had to leave the path, because of fallen trees. And all the time we climbed up and up, and the horses sweated and the sun beat hot on our backs. We rode with long, slack reins, and our shirts stuck to our backs, and Pete said, "Not much farther. My, it's hot."

We came to a clearing and there was a crash as a herd of deer disappeared in the undergrowth. There was a view on each side of us now, but the Millers wouldn't stop.

"Wait till you get to the view pole," they said. We left the clearing and followed another rocky winding path. We passed a spring, and Wendy said, "This is an old Indian trail, as old as the mountains I guess. It stretches all across Virginia right into Georgia."

I imagined Indians passing silently along the trail. "This part's got quite a history," Phil said.

We took down some rails and then we were on a wide

grass track. "We've reached the gas line," Wendy told us.

"This is the way our gas comes," Peter explained.

"It must have taken years to build it," Angus said.

"It goes down almost to the river," Wendy said.

Presently, we left the gas line and came to a sandy road.

"This takes you to the National Parks eventually," Phil told us.

"We generally bring the dogs with us when we come up here. But we can't now, because of the darned old rabies. The foxes have had a lot of it this summer," Wendy said.

"Gosh, how awful!" Angus exclaimed. "It's pretty dangerous, isn't it?"

"It sure is," Phil replied. "If you see a rabied cat, run for your life. If you're once bitten, you've just about had it."

"You can have an injection, but they don't always work. You generally end up a bit mental if you don't die of it," Wendy said.

I started watching the undergrowth on each side of the road for rabied bob cats and foxes.

"The cattle get it too. But they just get sick," Wendy continued.

"A month ago we didn't dare cross the back yard without a stick," Pete said.

"You mean on account of rabies?" Angus asked, and I noticed that he too was watching the undergrowth.

"Sure. The darned animals come right down off the mountains with it and infect our dogs and cats," Peter replied.

Wendy, who was leading, turned off the path on to a narrow trail. "We've nearly made it," she said. "Be ready for the finest view in the whole doggone United States of America."

We climbed a little hill and there we drew rein. We sat limply on our sweating horses. We seemed to have reached the top of the world. Below us, on all sides, stretched miles and miles of America. There were farms and villages, townships and towns, highways and dirt roads. There were railway lines running haphazard across the landscape; the Potomac river gleaming faintly in the sunlight. Beyond it all, were more mountains, blue and faint in the distance.

"You like it, huh?" Wendy asked.

"It's wonderful," I gasped. "Absolutely terrific."

"You can see the White House and the National Monument with binoculars from here on a fine day," Phil told us, with pride in his voice.

"And that's fifty miles away," Pete added.

We turned our horses and looked south, west, east and north, and on all sides the view was just as vast and breathtaking.

"It's super. I wish I had a camera," Angus said.

I was gazing at the view on the north side as he spoke, and suddenly I saw something moving, and it wasn't very far away. It was moving at a great speed and, as I watched, I realised that below us was a horse galloping riderless and alone. He moved beautifully with tremendous grace. His mane was windswept and his tail streamed behind him like a pennant in the breeze. He looked like something out of another world—beautiful, powerful and alone. "Look," I cried, pointing, "there's your wild horse." I felt terribly excited. He looked so beautiful alone in the valley.

It was ages before the others saw the wild horse. Then Phil said, "Yeah, there he goes. I wonder what happened to the two mares he had with him."

"Boy! Doesn't he look great? Wouldn't it be swell to own a nag like that?" Wendy cried.

Pete sat silent, his face set and determined. He obviously meant to catch that horse if it was the last thing he did on earth.

Angus's eyes were shining. "Isn't he wonderful, Jean?" he asked. "Just like a phantom horse."

"Has he got a name?" I said.

"Plenty. Some call him one thing, some another, but

24

hey're all bad," Phil replied, turning his dun. "Come n, let's go. And I shouldn't worship that horse, Jean," e added. "He's no saint."

We rode back along the sandy road; and Angus and I were full of the horse we had just seen. He was obviously a horse in a million, and I think that at that moment we were both determined that eventually he should be ours. How we would catch him when dozens of Virginians had failed was a question we didn't ask ourselves. Somehow,

A horse galloping riderless and alone

sometime we would tame him and then he would be ours for ever.

"Pity he was so far away," Phil said presently. "But maybe you'll see him nearer soon. He's a great horse."

We reached the gas line and now the sun was directly overhead. Frances felt weary. She obviously wasn't very fit and the long canter at the beginning had tired her.

We rode with slack reins, down and down until we reached the valley.

"We'll take you home," Wendy said. "That is, if you won't come back with us and eat whatever's going."

"I don't think we'd better. Our parents expect us," I replied, remembering Daddy's injunction about returning by one.

"It's been a lovely ride," Angus said. "Really super."

"You're very polite and English," Phil replied with a grin.

We jumped the wall again and I got left behind and jumped with the old-fashioned hunting seat. The bay mare cleared it beautifully this time, and Angus looked very pleased and patted her for ages.

"I guess we'll leave you now," Phil said.

"Well, thanks for a lovely ride," I replied.

"You're welcome. We'll be seeing you," the Millers said. They turned their horses, jumped the wall again and disappeared across the valley.

"You know we never thanked them for lending us the ponies; not properly anyway," I said.

"I shouldn't worry. I don't think Americans say thank you as much as we do. Didn't you see them grinning about me being polite?" Angus replied.

We unsaddled the horses and put them in the stable. We watered them and, finding that oats had been provided as well as everything else, we gave them each a feed.

I felt very stiff; in fact, my legs didn't seem to belong to me any more. I hadn't ridden since Easter.

Mummy had cooked some lunch. There was sweet corn, sweet potatoes and ham, followed by what we call over-stewed apples, and the Millers call apple sauce. As Angus and I ate, we told our parents about our ride and about the wild horse.

CHAPTER THREE

ANGUS AND I spent our first afternoon in Virginia grooming the ponies and helping our parents unpack. Most of the time our thoughts were with the wild horse and we were hopelessly forgetful. I put the butter in the breadbin and a pile of books in the kitchen cupboard. Angus couldn't remember where he had put anything and upset a bottle of ink over a pile of clean white handkerchiefs. Altogether, we weren't very popular with Mummy and Daddy.

After tea, which we made with tea bags, we turned the ponies out in the paddock. It was much cooler. The mountains were clear of mist, and Angus and I spent some time trying to work out where we had ridden in the morning. There was no sign of the wild horse.

Later, during the evening, Daddy took us all to a Drive-In Cinema, which is really just a cinema screen out of doors. You pay a dollar parking fee for your car and then sit and watch the film. There were hundreds of cars, full of teen-agers kissing, which Mummy said was disgusting at their age. The film was exciting, but otherwise rather awful, with lots of shooting, and film stars roughing it in the jungle without chipping their nail varnish or spoiling their hair-do's.

We ate scrambled eggs and spinach for supper, followed by peaches picked off the tree on the lawn.

I think I fell asleep that night as soon as my head touched the pillow. The last thing I remember hearing was the frogs singing. I dreamed about the film we had just seen. I was chasing an elephant called Joseph, which suddenly turned into the wild horse. A rabied lion appeared foaming at the mouth. I wanted to scream, but no sound came; then I heard the sound of hoofs and suddenly I knew the hoofs were real and all the rest a dream. I leapt from my bed and rushed to the window. A large moon lit up the mountains. The paddock was a mixture of light and shadow. Frances and the bay mare were standing alert in the moonlight, with heads high and pricked ears. I followed their gaze and saw a horse coming across the valley. He was moving beautifully with incredible ease. He looked very beautiful in the moonlight. I had no doubts as to his identity.

I dashed into Angus's room. As usual he was half-buried under the bedclothes. "Wake up, wake up," I shrieked into his ear, "the wild horse is here."

Angus sat up with a start; his dark hair on end, his eyes stupid with sleep. "What horse? Which horse?" he demanded. "I was dreaming of home. What are you doing roaming about in the middle of the night?"

I could have screamed with exasperation. In another moment, the wild horse might have vanished and we would have done nothing but gibber in a bedroom. "It's the wild horse," I repeated. "He's here in the paddock."

"You mean he's here?" yelled Angus, coming to life at last, and leaping from his bed. "Gosh, how super. Quick, there's no time to waste."

"Ssh. We don't want to wake up the whole house," I said, before tearing back to my own room and struggling into slacks and polo-necked jersey.

I ran into Angus at the top of the stairs, hitting my hip a violent blow on the banisters.

"Do look where you're going," cried Angus.

"What about you?" I asked, nursing my hip. "It takes two to make a collision.

"Ssh, there's Daddy coughing. Do come on," Angus hissed, as though I had started the argument.

We tore downstairs, through the kitchen and out into the bright moonlight. We made no plans. We ran straight to the paddock. For a moment we were thunderstruck. There, standing in our own paddock, was the wild horse. He was talking politely to Frances and the bay mare. I noticed that his shoulder was long and sloping and his hocks low to the ground.

"I'm going to get some oats and a halter. You never know, it might work," said Angus quietly.

"He must have jumped in," I said.

I could hear the frogs, and somewhere a cow was bellowing. Otherwise, everything was miraculously still.

Angus returned with oats in a bucket, and a halter concealed behind his back. We climbed the gate into the paddock with fast beating hearts. It seemed that our great chance had come.

Oh patient eyes, courageous hearts, I thought looking at the gold and flaxen horse before us.

"If only . . ." began Angus. Then the horse turned and saw us. He looked us up and down, but only for one split second; the next moment, he was galloping away across the paddock followed by the two mares. I felt a wild impulse to run after him, but restrained myself.

"Why didn't you rattle the oats?" I asked Angus angrily.

"It's a bit late to say that now," Angus retorted. "Here, you have them this time."

I took the oats; but I knew there wasn't going to be another time as we watched the wild horse galloping straight towards the wall, which was all that stood between him and freedom. I felt sick with disappointment, as I saw him prick his ears and lengthen his stride.

"He's going to jump," Angus cried, and started to run.

Another second and the Palomino was in the air and jumping alongside was the bay mare. Angus gave a cry of anguish. Frances refused and then neighed frantically. The wild horse didn't look back, but cantered on towards the mountains, followed by the bay mare. For a time, Angus and I ran desperately after them. But when our legs were aching and our hearts pounding, and the two horses were dots in the distance, we stopped and Angus said, "Supersonic! What are we to do now?"

"We've only got one horse left," I replied. "What will the Millers say?"

"Well, it isn't our fault. We did what we could," Angus said.

We turned dismally for home. The sound of the frogs was louder than ever, but the cow had stopped bellowing. Somewhere far away, a dog barked. I saw us sharing

Another second and the Palomino was in the air

Frances for the rest of the holidays, arguing about turns, riding and walking together across the hot, sun-baked Virginian countryside.

"Of all the bad luck! Why does it have to happen to us?" Angus exclaimed angrily.

"We'll *have* to catch him now," I said.

"But now with only one horse between us, I can't imagine," Angus replied.

We didn't speak again until we reached the paddock. Frances was cantering up and down the wall neighing in a heartbroken way. Mummy and Daddy were standing in the yard with overcoats over their pyjamas.

"Oh help! Why did they have to wake up?" asked Angus.

"Just our luck," I replied.

"What *is* happening?" Daddy called.

Angus and I explained what had happened. Our parents were very nice and not at all angry, though they hate us dashing about in the middle of the night.

We made tea in the kitchen and tried to decide what to do next. Daddy said that we should see the sheriff and ask him to organise a really big round up. Mummy thought Frances should be used to tempt the bay mare home. We ate hunks of bread-and-butter, and the sun appeared with the first light of dawn in the east.

"Perhaps the Millers will have a bright idea," Daddy said hopefully. "I suggest a return to bed. I'm due in Washington at ten o'clock."

Angus and I went back to bed with heavy hearts. I lay awake for ages, my head seething with pessimistic thoughts. I couldn't see how we would ever catch the wild horse. I wished that I was back in England with our own dear Moonlight and Mermaid to ride. I was much too hot in bed and being angry made me still hotter. I fell asleep at last to dream that the wild horse came into the kitchen and stole some cakes.

The sun was shining through my window when I wakened. I knew at once that I had slept late. I had a headache and felt fuddled with sleep.

I found Mummy in the kitchen. Daddy had already left for Washington. I made myself currant toast in the patent toasting machine, which jumps up toast when it's cooked, and Mummy boiled me an egg. Frances was standing desolately in the paddock resting one hind leg.

31

She obviously despaired of the bay mare's return. I started on my egg. Then the telephone bell rang.

Mummy said, "Go on eating. I'll answer it."

I wished that I had jeans to wear as I looked at the scorching day outside. I felt very cross and still rather sleepy.

Mummy returned. "It's the Millers for you," she said.

I suppose I shall have to explain about the bay mare, I thought, going reluctantly to the telephone.

Wendy answered when I picked up the receiver. "Hiya, Jean. Is that you?" she asked.

"Speaking," I replied.

"I hear you've lost the bay mare—too bad," Wendy continued. "That horse is getting a heck of a nuisance—time we did something."

She said it as though we just hadn't been trying to catch him up to now. "How did you know the mare had gone?" I asked.

"One of the farmhands saw her this morning. They were galloping across the valley together jumping the streams like two-year-olds. Boy, it makes me mad. Anyway, you're going to have my little roan, and I'm going to ride one of the work horses. We're coming right over," Wendy finished.

"We'll ride the work horse. Why should you?" I said, but Wendy had already rung off.

"They're coming right over," I told Mummy. "I'm going to wake Angus."

"It's going to be awfully hot for riding," Mummy said.

I wakened Angus and then I rushed outside to catch Frances. She was terribly pleased to see me and pushed her chestnut and white nose into the halter. I led her round to the stable and gave her a feed. Angus appeared munching currant loaf.

"What's this about having another horse?" he asked. I told him about Wendy ringing up and about the work horse. "I think the Millers are terribly generous. I expected them to be furious about the bay mare," I finished.

"Same here," Angus replied.

We groomed Frances and put on her tack. Then we heard hoofs. "Here they come," Angus said.

The Millers were in full force. "Hallo. How're you doing?" they called.

"Okay, thanks," we replied, leading Frances out of the stable.

"Here, you have my little roan, Jean," Wendy said. "You're smaller than Angus."

"I'll ride the work horse," I replied.

Phil laughed. "You'd look mighty funny perched up there," he said.

I argued, but to no avail. Wendy had decided that she would ride the work horse and nothing would change her decision.

"We thought we'd just hack round quietly this morning and make plans. It's too hot to go far," Phil said.

The work mare was called Sally. She was grey and similar to a Cleveland bay in build, though a little heavier.

The Millers told us more about the wild horse as we rode across the valley.

"He was reared by an English groom. That's why we thought he might take to you," Wendy said. "It wasn't until the groom left that the trouble started."

"We speak kind of English on account of Daddy coming from the old country. But we still speak with an American accent," Peter explained.

"He wasn't so wild at first. But everyone's chased him so much, that now he's as wild as they're made," Wendy told us.

"How long has he been loose?" Angus asked.

"Since March. He's only a four-year-old," Phil replied. "The English groom backed him around December when he was three and three-quarters. He had a heck of a time with him by all counts."

"Then at the end of February the groom died and after that he went from bad to worse. He's a mass of nerves they say," Wendy explained.

"I don't believe he's vicious at all," Phil said.

"But don't go thinking that if you catch him, you can ride him straight home, because you darned well can't," Pete told us. "He's some horse, that Palomino."

"He sounds it," Angus agreed.

"He's more a parade horse than anything else," Phil told us. "That's what they use Palominos for out in California. They wear beautiful Spanish saddlery and breastplates. But he's so darned fast they thought they'd try him on the race tracks."

"I guess he would have won a race or two," Pete said.

Wendy's roan, which I discovered was called Easter, was very handy. He was half cow pony and could turn on a sixpence, though he wasn't very well schooled by English dressage standards.

We rode back by the village and the Millers spent a dollar on chocolate. They pushed half of it into Angus's and my pockets. They seemed to imagine that we had been half-starved since birth in England. We parted by the post office.

"I don't believe we're ever going to catch that wild horse," said Angus dismally, as we rode the last piece home together. "The Millers don't seem to have any plans. We didn't really discuss it at all. We'll have to go on riding borrowed horses the whole time we're here. We'll never have a horse of our own. I know it's jolly nice of the Millers to lend us theirs and I'm being beastly and ungrateful, but riding borrowed ponies isn't like having one of your own. Is it?"

"Far from it," I agreed.

"I want to ride in gymkhanas and I don't believe the Millers ever go to shows," Angus said.

"You can't expect everything to go right from the word go. We've only been here three days," I reminded Angus.

34

"We'd better keep both the ponies in to-night," Angus said. "We can't afford to lose any more."

Angus and I washed up lunch and cleaned our tack during the afternoon. After tea, Daddy returned from Washington and suggested that we should all spend the next day there. Angus and I were horrified. We hate towns, and large towns like Washington most of all.

"Oh, need we? Must we? It's so super here," Angus wailed.

"And it's not as though we need to buy anything," I added, and I thought of trailing round crowded streets, beneath a pitiless sun.

"We thought you might like to see some of the sights. There's no need to shop. I want to buy a suit, that's all," Mummy said.

I was beginning to feel ungrateful. I wondered why grown-ups are always so keen on seeing sights. Then Daddy spoke, "Well, I don't see why you need come if you can stay and be sensible here. The point is, will you be sensible?" he asked.

"I don't see why we shouldn't be," Angus replied with hope in his voice. "Aren't we usually?"

"I doubt it. And anyway, this isn't England," Daddy replied.

"Will you promise to be sensible?" Mummy asked. "That means only riding very quietly, turning the cooker off when you've finished cooking, not speaking to strange men, and leaving the washing-up machine alone."

"And not going more than half a mile from the house," Daddy added.

"Yes. We'll eat only bread and cheese and apples and that will cut the cooker out. We won't use plates, so there will be no reason to use the washing-up machine. We'll only walk the ponies; and we'll avoid all strange men, black and white," Angus replied.

"And we'll be generally sensible," I added.

"And not go more than half a mile from the house," Daddy reminded us. "All right, you can stay."

Angus and I were delighted by our parents' decision, little knowing how later we would regret it. The Millers had told us that they would be spending the day visiting their grandmother in Maryland. Angus and I visualised a wonderfully peaceful time by ourselves, and we made all sorts of plans between tea and supper. "We can spend the morning schooling quietly in the paddock. I want to try Wendy's roan and I'm sure I'm not too heavy for him, if we only walk and trot," Angus said.

"And we can muck out the stable and give the ponies a really good groom," I added.

"Well, don't get kicked," Mummy told us.

"Or spike yourselves with pitchforks," Daddy said.

"We'll be terribly careful," Angus promised.

"If anything goes wrong, ring up Daddy. We'll give you the number," Mummy told us.

Angus and I retired to bed that night feeling very gay. To-morrow would be our first day in Virginia without the Millers' company and, though we liked them, a day alone appealed to us as a pleasant change. The last thing Angus said to me before we parted for the night, was, "One great advantage Virginia has over England is that you can depend upon it being fine." I was to remember that remark later, but at the time I just said, "Which is really rather super."

CHAPTER FOUR

THE NEXT day dawned clear and fine as expected. The sky was a true undiluted blue. Life seemed suddenly wonderful to us all.

We ate breakfast together in the kitchen—an English breakfast of bacon and eggs, followed by toast and marmalade. Our parents left for Washington at nine-thirty, after giving us fresh instructions about behaving sensibly. As the car disappeared along the dirt road, Angus said, "Come on, let's ride."

We had mucked out the two loose-boxes earlier.

"We can groom the ponies after we've ridden. They're sure to be hot and dirty by then," Angus said, as we hurried to the stable.

We put our clean tack on the ponies. "I'll start on Easter, if you don't mind," Angus told me.

"That's all right by me," I replied gaily. I was feeling stupidly happy and carefree. I think Angus was too.

"I really didn't think Virginia could be so super, did you?" Angus asked.

"No, I dreaded coming at times, in spite of what everyone told me at school. Of course, I still like England best," I replied, remembering Sparrow Cottage in August with the sun casting shadows across the lawn, and the sound of church bells coming across the fields, and the mad, winding English roads.

"We really must write home about Mermaid and Moonlight soon. We haven't written to anyone since we've been here," Angus said.

"We'd better lead the ponies out into the paddock and then mount. We don't want to fall off trying to open the gate," I said.

"I wish Mummy and Daddy hadn't made so many

stipulations. It's really rather tiresome. I mean just walking the ponies will get jolly boring after a time," Angus grumbled.

"I don't think they really meant us only to walk. I think they meant that we weren't to do anything silly," I replied, opening the paddock gate.

"Well, I'm jolly well going to trot," Angus said, mounting Easter.

It was very hot in the paddock. We walked for a few minutes; then we tightened our girths and trotted.

Angus, like most boys, soon tired of schooling. "Let's ride outside. It's too hot to do anything in here. Easter's dripping with sweat already," he said.

It *was* hot too—a sultry, ominous heat quite unlike anything we had yet met in Virginia.

We walked along the dirt road and then, after opening a gate, into the valley.

"We mustn't forget about the half mile. It would be awful if something happened when we were miles from home," I told Angus.

"I'm not suggesting that we should ride far. I'm just tired of riding round and round that paddock," Angus replied.

It was cooler in the valley. A faint breeze blew from the mountains; the Hereford cattle had vanished in search of shade. Nothing seemed to stir.

"I knew it would be cooler here. I wish we could ride in the mountains," Angus said.

"I'm jolly glad I'm not in Washington. Think of looking at statues and monuments to-day," I said.

"It would be the end," Angus agreed.

The ponies went well together. They were obviously old friends.

"Daddy says we've got to start seeing about schools next week," Angus told me.

I didn't answer. I had just seen two horses moving across the valley. "Look!" I cried. "Angus, look! There

38

they are—the Palomino and the bay mare. They're heading straight for the mountains."

They were quite near, jogging along together beneath the scorching sun.

"Gosh, you're right. What a stroke of luck," Angus cried.

Forgotten were all our parents' instructions, as we turned our ponies towards the mountains. Frances and Easter joined in the spirit of the chase. They galloped as though our lives depended on their speed.

"This may be our big chance," Angus said.

We gained steadily on the two horses, until they heard our pounding hoofs; then they broke into a gallop and Frances started to blow a little, and Angus said, "I hope this pony can stand my weight," and patted Easter's neck.

We jumped a wall and a "coop" almost without noticing. We reached a trail and were galloping up hill, with trees on each side of us, and constant twists and turns. It was tremendously exciting. "We may not be gaining, but we aren't losing ground either," Angus cried. "Oh, if only we can catch them."

The mountains were very still, except for the sound of our pounding hoofs and an occasional sharp ring as horseshoe met rock. At first, we passed cattle standing in the midst of undergrowth, their white faces besieged by flies; but gradually we left even these behind and the trail became narrower still and far more rocky. And then the Palomino left the trail, and we were galloping amid trees, banging our knees and our heads. Frances and Easter were marvellous. They twisted and turned, missing trees by inches. The ground was strewn with boulders and they jumped some, avoided others, and stumbled recklessly over the rest. In a few moments we were lost in a world of trees, and it was then that I remembered the instructions that our parents had given us before leaving for Washington. I felt suddenly sick then and there was a lump in my throat.

"We shouldn't be here," I yelled to Angus, who was

leading. "Don't you remember what Mummy and Daddy said?"

There was a pause before Angus replied, and I realised how completely we were lost.

"It's a bit late to think of that now. For all we know we may be heading straight for a dead end. We can't afford to miss a chance," Angus replied.

I think the devil must have possessed us then. For we galloped recklessly on, when it would have been so easy to turn back and find our own way home. Afterwards, Angus always said that it was his fault, that I had wanted to turn back. But that wasn't true. I could have spoken then or ridden home alone. I wanted to go on just as much as Angus did.

We left the trees at last, and started to gallop down an old ravine; and now the sound of falling boulders was added to that of galloping hoofs, as the horses slipped and slid, keeping their balance only by a miracle. I shut my eyes and wished that Frances had a longer neck and a better shoulder. And then it happened.

"My saddle's slipping," Angus yelled. There was panic in his voice, which echoed amid the mountains.

"Hang on to his mane," I cried, and my voice echoed too and came back to us. I had an awful sense of calamity for a few terrible seconds. Easter's head seemed to disappear between his knees. I could see Angus and the saddle disappearing with it. It was a moment I shall never forget. I saw Angus hit the rocks and the boulders, and Easter jump him and go on. I only just stopped Frances in time.

Angus lay horribly still on his side with one arm stretched across his face. I dismounted and Frances snorted and started to back away. She obviously had no intention of standing while I examined Angus. Fortunately there was a tree quite near; saying lots of words we're not allowed to use, I tied her to it and returned to my brother. He was breathing, though his face looked white and lifeless. I cried, "Angus, Angus, wake up,"

ut without avail. There was no sound but the echo of
my own plaintive voice. I knelt down and felt Angus
all over in search of broken bones. I found nothing. But
I didn't dare move him, because for all I knew his back
might be broken, or his neck, or his pelvis. My know-
ledge of first aid was very small, but I did know that
people can break bones without them showing except in

Easter's head seemed to disappear between his knees

X-rays, and I wasn't going to kill my brother by moving
him.

But I had to do something. The sky had become over-
cast while we had recklessly pursued the two horses; a
faint ominous breeze stirred the trees. I didn't know
where I was, nor the way home. I didn't even know the
time. Easter had disappeared in pursuit of the two horses.
There was only one thing to do and that was to find

41

help. Wishing that I had a coat to put over Angus, untied Frances and mounted. I tightened her girths and taking one last look at my brother, I made a detour and rode on down the ravine.

I couldn't forget what our parents had said: their words haunted me, as I hurried Frances—we had promised to be sensible, we had promised to ride quietly, we had broken nearly all our promises.

Although I hurried Frances, it was ages before we came to any clearing and then it was one I had never seen before. By this time, I had decided to leave the way home to Frances. I was lost more completely than I had ever been lost before.

The sky had grown darker and in the distance there sounded the first depressing roll of thunder. Frances was marvellous: she never hesitated about which path to follow; she seemed quite tireless. I tried to memorise our journey. My mind was full of lefts and rights, of odd shaped trees and sudden turns. And then the first sheet of lightning shot across the sky—lightning quite unlike anything I had ever seen before. It was long and jagged, and, for one awful moment, it lit up the whole sky, thunder followed and then the heaviest deluge of rain I've ever experienced. Frances stopped and stood shivering. The trees seemed to tremble; the sound of falling rain blotted out everything, until the next roll of thunder came and the same terrible flash of lightning.

I thought of Angus lying unprotected in the ravine. Already I was soaked to the skin. I forced Frances on into the blinding rain, down and down until the trail was suddenly familiar and I could see light ahead. I knew then that in a moment we would reach the valley. I had already decided that I would find my way to the Millers' farm. I hoped that I would find farmhands who would come to my assistance; though how we would get Angus down from the mountain I had no idea.

We reached the valley as fresh thunder crashed and more rain fell. My shoes were overflowing with water. My hair was plastered to my face. But I could have cheered as I caught a glimpse of what I guessed was the Millers' farm through the rain.

We galloped down a hill; and scrambled over a wall, where the ground was under two inches of water. The fields were deserted. The streams were running over the drive. The farmyard was empty. Only a lone cream convertible was parked by the house. I think I started to cry then, and my tears fell with the rain into France's chestnut and white mane.

I rode madly round the farmyard yelling "Help, help. Is anyone at home?" For a moment I felt quite mad; then I heard the faint sound of chopping coming from a small shed at the back of the house. I threw Frances's reins over a gate and ran towards it yelling, "Help, help. There's been an accident."

I fell over a stone and scrambled to my feet again. I didn't notice that blood was pouring from one of my hands. All I could see was Angus lying white and still in the ravine.

I found a lean, middle-aged man chopping wood. I poured out my story without stopping for breath.

"He may be dying by now," I finished, voicing my worst fears. "Please, please can you help?"

"You're a Britisher, I guess. I can tell that by your voice," the man said, putting down his chopper. "I don't know how we'll get your brother off the mountains; it'll be real hard. If Mr. Miller was at home . . ."

"Haven't you got anything which can get up there?" I asked. "A jeep or a tractor?"

"We have a tractor," the man said slowly. "Wait a bit and I'll find Charlie. He's the only one that can start it."

I waited in agony while he disappeared in search of Charlie. It was still raining. A century seemed to pass, before the farm hand returned accompanied by Charlie, who was younger and had two fingers missing from his left hand.

"So there's been an accident," he said, looking at me "I'll sure do my best for you; but I can't promise to ge the tractor up there, not on the ground as it is."

It didn't seem to matter to them that someone migh be dying up in the mountains. They didn't hurry much Perhaps they thought I was just a panicky child, who go excited over nothing.

It was ages before the tractor started. The sky wa quite clear by then and the sun was shining. The mer hitched what they called a drag behind the tractor. It was made of wood and resembled a sledge. I collected some old coats and a couple of horse rugs, from the saddle room, to put over Angus. I felt calm in a horribly despairing way. Everything had taken hours. I had put Frances in a loose-box; and rung up the doctor Charlie suggested. I had found a negro cook in the Millers' kitchen and she had promised to have hot blankets and hot-water bottles waiting for Angus when he returned; also hot tea with plenty of sugar in it. She had given me a flask of brandy to pour down his throat. I had meant to ring up Daddy, but his number was in the kitchen at Mountain Farm, and I didn't think of ringing up inquiries or the British Embassy.

Charlie drove the tractor, I opened the necessary gates. Ages seemed to pass before we reached the edge of the mountains. There was a rainbow across the sky and the trail smelt wonderful. Charlie and the other man, who was called Joe, whistled and asked me whereabouts I came from and whether I liked America, I answered "Oxfordshire" and "Yes." I was too worried for polite conversation.

I asked Joe the time, and he replied, "Two o'clock." That meant that Angus had been lying for more than two hours soaked to the skin in the ravine.

Soon we reached a place where the tractor could go no farther.

"What now?" the men asked.

I wished that we had brought a stretcher of some sort; an old gate or a hurdle would have done.

"We'd better take the strongest horse rug and carry him back in that," I replied.

We left the tractor and I led the way. The men followed with the horse rug. It was very hot. The sky was quite cloudless; even the rainbow had disappeared. It was difficult to realise that there had just been a storm. Several times I took the wrong path and we had to turn back. Fortunately, the hoofprints Frances had made coming down were still visible.

At last we reached the bottom of the ravine.

"He's half-way up. Only a little way now," I cried to the men.

I wondered how we would find Angus, as I struggled up the ravine, slipping and sliding on the boulders. Supposing he had regained consciousness, I thought suddenly, and started to find his own way home? The men were puffing behind. My legs felt horribly weak. I started to run. Supposing he's dead, I thought.

Angus was still lying there on his side, just as I had left him. In spite of the sun, his face looked purple with cold.

"He's quite a little guy then," Charlie said.

"He looks real bad. How long has he been lying here?" Joe asked.

"Hours and hours," I muttered, noticing that Angus still breathed. "That's why I wanted you to hurry." I felt like crying again. I think I was nearly exhausted.

We rolled Angus carefully in the horse rug. Then we started back down the ravine.

"Do you think they'll take him straight to hospital?" I asked the men.

"I guess so. He looks real bad to me," Joe replied.

"Lying up there in the rain won't have done him a lot of good," Charlie said.

We came to the tractor and laid Angus carefully on the drag. I covered him with coats. Charlie started the engine.

Then we began our journey down. Joe and I eased th
drag over the rocks and held Angus. Even so, it wa
a horribly bumpy journey. We didn't talk much. I thin
the men were terribly upset now that they had seer
Angus.

We came at last to the valley, and the Millers' romantic
house basking in the sunshine. We could see a black ca
parked alongside the convertible.

"That'll be Doc," Charlie said.

Then I saw another car and I couldn't believe my eyes
because it should have been in Washington. It was our
car and nearby was an anxious crowd, staring towards
the mountains. I ran forward and opened the last gate, and
Daddy and Mummy ran to meet me. "How badly is he
hurt?" they cried.

The doctor came forward then and started to examine
Angus. Mummy explained that she and Daddy had rung
Mountain Farm several times between twelve and two;
getting no reply they had become anxious and telephoned
the Millers. The coloured cook Annie had answered and
told them about the accident.

"After that we came here just as fast as we could,"
Mummy finished.

The doctor stood up. "As far as I can judge there are
no bones broken. But I'd like to get him to hospital
under observation. I can take him in my automobile I
guess. I don't think we need an ambulance," he said.

"You'd better stay here, Jean," Daddy said. "Annie
says she'll look after you till the Millers get back. We'll
fetch you just as soon as we're through with the hospital."
They lifted Angus into the doctor's car, and wrapped him
in rugs.

"We'll ring you as soon as there's any news," Mummy
said.

"Don't worry. He'll make out all right," the doctor
said, patting me on the head.

Daddy thanked Charlie and Joe. Annie appeared and
invited me in for a "A real hot cup of coffee."

No one asked why Angus and I were riding in the mountains, instead of within half a mile of Mountain Farm.

The cars drove away. The men returned to their work. Suddenly everything was very still. I followed Annie into the kitchen.

CHAPTER FIVE

THE MILLER'S kitchen was large with windows on both sides: the floor was tiled, there was an open fireplace, a long table, and numerous cupboards, as well as two sinks, an electric cooker and a washing-up machine. Next to the kitchen was the laundry, which housed the deep freeze, two refrigerators, a sink and a Bendix washing machine.

Annie was slim; her hair was permed. She was not at all like the old negro mammies one sees so often in films. She sat me down at the kitchen table, and fetched coffee, and put steak under the grill and corn on to cook.

"I'm going to give you a proper meal. You must be real hungry," she said.

I felt in a daze and very miserable. I don't think there's anything quite as bad as a really guilty conscience. I knew that soon the Millers would be home and then I should have to confess to losing Easter as well as the bay mare. Sometime I should have to tell my parents a dismal tale of stupidity and broken promises. To me at that moment the future looked horribly black, even supposing Angus wasn't seriously hurt.

Annie was very kind. She offered me cigarettes and cake. She turned the wireless on and we listened to popular music until the steak and corn were cooked. When I started to eat, I found that I was ravenous. Annie left me and started to iron in the laundry. Outside, the sun

shifted to the west. I could see a lake, the Millers' long
drive; and the Hereford cattle coming down from the
mountains. I decided that Angus must have reached the
hospital, and I imagined bustling nurses, and doctors in
white coats. Then a car door banged and Annie hurried
outside. I guessed the Millers had returned, and suddenly
I couldn't eat any more.

But it was a long time before anyone came into the
kitchen; not until I had washed up my coffee cup, and
the plate and knife and fork I had dirtied. I had made
friends with a smiling Dalmatian by then, and I was
quite sick with apprehension.

The Millers all came in together and I knew instinctively
that they had been told about the accident.

"Hallo, Jean, it's nice to see you," they said. They were
all rather well-dressed. Mrs. Miller and Wendy were in
summer dresses and strollers. Phil and Pete were attired
in suits. Mr. Miller wore a checked coat and grey trousers.
It was the first time I had seen them in anything but
jeans. Looking back, I suppose I must have looked a
pitiful figure in comparison. My face was tear stained
and my hand had bled all over the aertex shirt I had
chosen so gaily in the morning.

"We're so upset to hear about Angus. But don't worry,
Jean, I'm sure he'll make out all right," Mrs. Miller said
reassuringly.

"It's wonderful what people get over. You think they're
gonners and the next moment you meet them riding like
the devil as though nothing had ever happened," Mr.
Miller told me.

"You're sharing my room," Wendy said, and she
sounded pleased.

"But am I staying?" I asked. I felt in a muddle. Everyone seemed to be talking at once, and I wanted to confess
about Easter.

"Of course you are. You're staying just as long as Angus
is ill," Mr. Miller replied.

I wasn't sure that I wanted to stay. I wanted to talk to

Mummy and Daddy about the accident, and visit Angus in hospital, and sleep in my own bed at Mountain Farm.

"And we're all delighted to have you," said Phil, smiling.

"Come and see our room. I'm sure you'll love it," Wendy told me.

"Daddy's going to ring up soon. And I've lost Easter," I confessed with a rush. "He's got all his tack on—that's the awful part."

I felt like crying. The Millers didn't seem to realise how awful the day had been. They were cheerful and kind; but I wanted someone who would say that everything hadn't been my fault, that no one could have done more than I had, that they were certain Angus would soon recover and that Easter would come home.

"Don't you worry about that. Easter can look after himself," Mr. Miller replied, patting me on the back.

"We'll start thinking about him to-morrow," Mrs. Miller said.

"But shouldn't we look for him? He might get hung up or something," I said.

The Millers laughed. "Not him. It's not the first time he's spent a night on the mountains," Wendy answered.

Then the telephone rang. "That's for me," I cried, running into a spacious hall hung with sporting prints.

"It's in the room on the right," Phil called.

I found the telephone, but it wasn't Daddy. A voice said, "I'm calling about a spot of trouble we've been having with some moonshiners in the mountains. Is that Mr. Miller?"

"No, I'll fetch him," I replied, and fled back to the kitchen.

I was terribly disappointed. Wendy took me to her room, which like the kitchen had windows on both sides. There were two beds, lots of furniture, a television set and a wireless. The beds had gay counterpanes and the curtains were made of checked gingham.

"How do you like it?" Wendy asked.

"It's super," I replied, and then I sat down on the nearest bed and started to cry.

Wendy didn't know what to do. She shut all the windows and turned over some papers on a desk. She put away a pair of jeans which were lying on the floor. Then she said:

"Don't worry, Jean. I know your brother's going to be all right. Of course he is," but she didn't sound at all certain.

"The awful part is we weren't supposed to ride farther than half a mile from the house," I confessed; and then I told her the whole story.

When I had finished Wendy said, "We all do silly things sometimes in our lives. You were just unlucky. Boy, when I think of some of the things I've done. . . . Far worse things than riding farther than I was told. Honestly, Jean, I've got away with murder. Don't you know the saying, *Who never makes mistakes never makes anything.* Daddy is always quoting it."

As Wendy spoke, I decided that she was a great deal nicer than I had suspected. Then the telephone started to ring.

"That must be Daddy," I cried, leaping to my feet. I felt horribly weak as I ran downstairs. I didn't dare imagine what Daddy might have to say.

Mr. Miller was speaking, "Yes, she's still here. We thought she might stay the night. Sure. No trouble at all. Here, it's for you," he said, handing me the receiver.

"Hallo, is that Jean?" Daddy asked.

"I could hear my heart beating. "Yes," I answered, and my voice came out very small. "How's Angus?"

"Much better. He's conscious. He's to stay here for another twenty-four hours, but they can't find any broken bones or anything. He can't remember a thing, but he's quite cheerful now and asking about you."

I felt immensely relieved; nothing mattered much now that I knew Angus was recovering.

50

"Are you all right?" Daddy continued. "Charlie has kindly said that you can stay for a bit."

"I'm quite all right, thank you. And terribly pleased about Angus," I replied.

"Here's Mummy," Daddy said.

"Hallo, isn't it wonderful about Angus?" Mummy asked. "We're terribly pleased. Are you all right?"

"Yes, quite okay," I said.

"We're going to stay here overnight," Mummy told me. "We hope to bring Angus back quite soon. The doctor doesn't want him moved until he's got over the concussion. At present he's lying in a darkened room."

"I'm terribly sorry it happened," I apologised.

"We can't see how it did," Mummy replied cheerfully. "Never mind, you can explain it all later. The great thing is Angus is okay."

A few minutes later, Mummy rang off.

"Is he all right?" Mrs. Miller asked.

I told the Millers everything my parents had said. Then Phil introduced me to the dogs: Cop, the Dalmatian I had already met; Maggie, a little cairn; and Susie, a sweet fox terrier with a large patch of black over one eye. They all seemed to belong to everyone. Pete had disappeared. Outside a breeze stirred the apple trees, which were scattered at intervals across the lawn. The sun was setting. A jeep full of farm men was disappearing along the drive.

"To-morrow we'll have a round up. We can't miss the opportunity of having Jean here," Mr. Miller said.

"But what about the horses? We haven't got enough to go round now?" Wendy replied. "Frances must rest to-morrow, she's dog tired."

I thought of the bay mare and Easter roaming the mountains together.

"What's wrong with old Pelican?" Mr. Miller asked.

"But he hasn't been ridden for such a heck of a long time," Wendy replied.

"It'll do him good to have some work," Mr. Miller answered.

"Jean can have my mare. I don't mind riding Pelican," Phil said.

"I shall ride Sally," Wendy told us.

I couldn't see myself riding Phil's dun mare. But I didn't say anything. I felt I must ride who I was told, particularly since Angus and I were responsible for the loss of two horses already.

The Millers were terribly kind. At dinner they gave me the best piece of the rib roast and afterwards when everybody drank coffee I was provided with a cup of tea. Pete gave me a large box of chocolates, which he had bought in the village, while I was being introduced to the dogs. Phil presented me with one of his fountain pens; and Wendy showed me all her horsy books which weren't in my bedroom at Mountain Farm.

After we had eaten, we all watched television in Wendy's room. I thought I wouldn't sleep; but when eventually I retired to bed, some time between eleven and twelve, I fell asleep immediately and didn't dream at all.

Morning came bright and early in Wendy's room. A light breeze stirred the checked curtains, lazy clouds drifted across a blue sky; I could hear the men fetching the cows and the singing of the frogs in the low land. Wendy was still sleeping, with one arm tangled in her red-brown hair. Birds were arguing in the apple trees on the lawn; the lake and streams shone silver and gold in the sunlight. I could hear Annie putting the kettle on to boil in the kitchen. Someone was running taps in the bathroom. I couldn't bear to stay in bed a moment longer. I dressed quickly and hurried downstairs.

I found Annie breaking eggs into a basin. She said "Do you like waffles? Mrs. Miller says I make them good, real good. She says Annie make waffles for breakfast 'cos all the children love your waffles, and I don't suppose Jean's ever had them before." Annie's black face was wreathed in smiles.

"No, never. I've always wanted to try them too. How super," I said.

I wandered outside. Secretly, I hoped that Easter would have returned, but there was no sign of him. Pete was catching the horses.

"Hallo, Jean," he called. "You're up early. The others are still in bed." Pete was unusually gay. "I'm crazy about the early morning. It's the finest part of the day. When I've finished with school and college I'm going to farm," he told me.

Pete whistled for the horses and they trotted across the paddock. He had the three dogs at his heels. We led the horses in with just our arms round their necks. When they were all in the stables, we gave them each a feed of oats.

Pete said, "I bet Phil's mad. He hates round-ups. I'm the only one who cares about them."

I was seeing Pete in a new light. He seemed a different person by himself. He hadn't Phil's glamorous good looks—Phil, one could imagine being a film star, a dashing officer in uniform, a pilot, a racing motorist—but he cared more about things. I knew that Pete would rather die than part with an old favourite. He would hang on to a farm he loved obstinately in the face of extreme poverty. Money would mean little to Pete, beyond new fences for his farm, I decided.

We watched the horses eating. "I'm going to send my chestnut mare to stud. I think she should breed a nice foal," Pete said.

Pelican was a lean, grey horse with a wall eye. He was heavily scarred, and he watched us warily out of his good eye, as he munched his feed.

"He's never been much good. He's too darned cunning," Pete told me.

We ate breakfast in the long dining-room where we had eaten supper the night before. There were waffles and bacon, loads of home-made bread and dairy butter. Phil hardly ate anything. Pete devoured nine waffles;

53

Wendy ate mostly bread. I tried the waffles, eating them in the traditional manner with butter, syrup and bacon. Personally, I like them better without the bacon, which I didn't think mixed well with the syrup. As we ate we discussed the round-up. We were to start by riding to given spots in the mountains. There was some argument as to which horses we were to ride. I remained silent. I was now suddenly determined to ride Pelican. Once we had reached our given spots, we were to ride down, driving any cattle we met before us.

"They're never much trouble till you reach the lower meadows, Jean. Then they're a heck of a lot," Mr. Miller told me.

"We drive them all in, and separate them afterwards in the loading pens," Peter explained.

"The men will all be waiting for you at the field gate," Mr. Miller said.

We carried the breakfast things through to the kitchen and put them in the washing-up machine, before hurrying to the stable yard. The horses had finished eating. I decided to take the bull by the horns. "I'm riding Pelican," I stated firmly. "It's my fault you are two horses short. It's quite obvious that I'm the person who should ride him, and anyway I'd just as soon ride him as the dun mare." I said it with rather a rush; and Phil began to laugh.

"You sound as though you've made up your mind all right," he said.

"But you know he's a bit of a rogue, Jean, don't you?" Pete asked, and he sounded worried.

"I don't care. I'm going to ride him," I replied. Phil shrugged his shoulders. "When women make up their minds . . ." he said.

"We don't want another accident," Pete said.

"Suits me all right, I'd much rather ride my dun," Phil told us, whistling gaily.

"What does Pelican do, anyway?" I asked Pete. "He doesn't look vicious."

"One never knows. I think he's nuts," Pete replied.

We collected our tack from the saddle room. I had the choice of a gag and curb, or a pelham. I turned them both down and chose a snaffle. I think the Millers were rather surprised. I explained that my hands weren't particularly good, and that I had been told often that difficult horses were happiest in snaffles. I refused the offer of a martingale. If Pelican's neck had been strong and heavy I don't know which bridle I would have chosen. But he didn't look like a puller. He looked more like a horse which would go behind his bit and rear.

We didn't bother to groom the horses. Pete helped me bridle Pelican. Then we led the horses out and mounted. Pelican felt tall and bony. I could feel him watching me with his good eye, and his ears were back.

"Be careful, Jean. He reared here once," Pete said.

"I'm glad I chose this old plug. I love her," Wendy told us, patting Sally.

Pelican followed the other horses with short uneasy steps. I gave him his head and hoped that nothing would go wrong. I didn't wish to be in hospital as well as Angus, and Pete's obvious anxiety made me wonder what Pelican had done in the past to earn himself such a bad name.

It was a wonderful day. There were still clouds in the sky, and a light breeze fanned our faces as we rode across the valley. Pelican started to relax and the Millers ceased to watch me anxiously. I felt like singing. I loved Virginia at that moment, and the sound of hoofs on the hard track, and the lovely view of the dreaming mountains already turning red and green in places, but still romantic, wild and full of adventure. Mummy has often complained that I never learn from bitter experience. She says that I'm an incurable adventuress and will come to a sticky end. I think she must be right, because I remember that at that moment I longed for an exciting chase through the mountains more than anything else, in spite of the awful things which had happened only the day before.

When we came to the mountains, we parted, each taking his own trail.

"Be seeing you," we called to one another, and "Best of luck."

Pete helped me bridle Pelican

My trail was one of the loveliest; the ground was soft and green, the sun shone through the trees, lighting the undergrowth with gold. Pelican's stride became long and free.

I sang as I rode up and up into the mountains, songs like "Old Faithful," "She'll be Coming Round the Mountain" and "When it's Springtime in the Rockies." I didn't feel like an exile. I felt terribly at home with the

reak of leather, reins between my fingers, and Pelican's
rey ears cocking backwards and forwards as he listened to
ny songs.

CHAPTER SIX

WHEN I reached my turning point, I had already passed
several cattle. Pelican was sweating, and the sun was
much hotter. I hoped that Angus wasn't too hot in hospital;
then I remembered that I was in America and every
hospital was sure to have an air conditioner. I was
sorry that he was missing the round-up, because it's the
sort of thing he loves. I imagined him in a very clean
bed eating grapes and reading magazines.

Pelican was pleased to turn round and start back down
the trail. We made several detours to collect cattle and
soon we had a herd of five or six in front of us. Pelican
was marvellous. He plunged willingly into the most awful
clumps of brambles and was far handier than I had
expected. I felt like a real cowboy as gradually my herd
grew; and I decided that some day I would take a job
on a ranch and round up cattle from dawn to dusk. Later
I was to learn that jeeps have replaced horses to a large
extent in the Wild West, and that being a cowboy is terribly exhausting, particularly in winter. But now, as my
herd grew and grew, I was happy with my illusions and I
whistled gaily as I rode down towards the valley.

And then, quite suddenly, I heard hoofs. At first I
thought it must be one of the Millers coming for help.
Then a neigh echoed through the mountains and jumping
the undergrowth came three horses—the bay mare, Easter;
and our phantom horse the Palomino. Pelican threw up
his head. The cattle stopped. Time seemed to stand still.
Easter's saddle was half under his stomach; his martingale
was dangling; his bridle had disappeared. They snorted

57

when they saw the cattle, and sniffed the air. East
looked peculiar without his bridle—like a person wh
wears spectacles, suddenly appearing without them.

Pelican whinnied and the three horses advanced slowl
I held my breath. I could hear Phil calling to his catt
in the valley. A grey squirrel crossed the trail. My her
started to move. The three horses looked at Pelican; the
skirted the cattle and began to walk on towards the valle
I felt like cheering them. I now had a herd of cattle an
three horses. If only they'd remain quiet and calm when w
reached the open, I might have a chance, I decided. Th
Palomino looked wonderful leading us all. The sun shon
on his gold coat and flaxen mane and tail; he walke
with a long, effortless stride. The other horses had to jo
to keep up with him and the cattle ambled behind, bellow
ing and mooing at intervals. I felt very happy and trium
phant. I knew no one else could have collected a herd
like mine, and the vicious Pelican was behaving
beautifully.

We reached the valley and I saw other herds approaching the allotted field. I could see that Pete and I were
destined to meet quite soon. Everyone started to shout
and cheer when they saw me. The Palomino, Easter and
the bay mare threw up their heads and I started to hurry
the cattle. I didn't want to lose them, now that we were so
near the field; most of all I didn't want to lose the three
horses. Wendy was coming round the corner of the valley;
her herd looked enormous with at least half a dozen young
heifers, as well as young bulls and cows and calves. Mr.
and Mrs. Miller and Joe and Charlie were spread out by
the field gate. The Palomino broke into a canter, Easter
and the bay mare followed. The cattle started to run
awkwardly after them.

"Take them slowly," I heard Pete call. "You'll never
get them in that way."

But, quite suddenly, my herd was out of control. The
Palomino was leading it away from the gate and the
people waiting in the valley. The three horses were

alloping in front, their manes and tails flying, their hoofs leaving a trail of dust behind them. I knew I had to turn them. It was no good Pete yelling, "Take them slowly." A few more minutes dallying and my herd would be lost. I pushed Pelican into a gallop, and there was dust in my eyes and my mouth; it stuck to my face and shirt, to Pelican's grey coat. It was everywhere and in the midst of it were my cattle galloping madly in pursuit of the three horses. I urged Pelican faster. His ears were back; he felt as though years had passed since he had last been asked to gallop. But he did his best, and soon we had passed the cattle and were gaining steadily on Easter. The Palomino was outstripping us all. And then from another direction came Phil. His dun mare was dark with sweat; he carried a hunting whip and he was yelling, "Back, back. Get back."

I hoped he didn't mean me. I had no intention of turning back at that moment. I urged Pelican faster. I thought how lovely the Palomino looked, and wondered whether he would look the same when he wasn't wild any more, when Angus and I had him standing in the stable at Mountain Farm. I was alongside Easter now. We had reached the low-lying land. I passed Easter, and the ground was squelchy under Pelican's hoofs, and I could hear the frogs singing endlessly. The cattle were no longer with us. Instead of dust, there was mud in my face, and flying stones. Phil was gaining; another moment, and he was in front of the Palomino. The horses turned and I turned too, almost colliding with Phil.

"Great work," he cried. "We'll have the darned horse yet."

And now we were galloping towards the gate and the people waiting. Pete had collected my cattle, making one gigantic herd. Wendy was moving slowly across the valley. I wondered who would have the wild horse if we caught him now. I didn't want to share him with the Millers. I wanted to have a horse of our own looking out of the loose-boxes at Mountain Farm.

Easter was already giving in. We had to keep drivin
him otherwise he would have been trotting on his ow
behind the others.

As we drew near the gate, Wendy and Pete left the
herds to come to our assistance. Poor Pelican was nearl
finished; he was almost gasping for breath.

"Let them come in slowly. Gently does it," Mr. Mille
called.

We were nearly there. Phil's herd was already in th
paddock. Charlie and Joe were smiling and gesticulatin
with large sticks.

The bay mare and Easter broke into a trot. The
looked exhausted; Easter's saddle was plastered with mud
his stirrups and leathers were missing.

"Boy, if only we can get them all in," Wendy shouted.

Pete's face was grim and determined.

"Come on now, let's see what you can do," Charlie
called.

The Palomino was eyeing the gate warily, and now no
one spoke. The vital moment had come. The three horses
all broke into a walk. Pete, Phil, Wendy and I edged
closer. Back in the valley, Pete's herd was slowly returning to the mountains.

We moved forward cautiously, and quite suddenly the
bay mare took the lead and walked fearlessly into the
paddock; Easter followed. We waited in silence for the
Palomino to follow. He stopped and gazed at the landscape; he stood very erect and sniffed the air. My heart
seemed to stand still. Another moment and he might be
ours. And then he made up his mind. He turned on his
hocks and faced us, and Phil cried, "Get back, will you.
Get back." and cracked his whip. The men rushed forward with their sticks.

Wendy screamed, "Quick. Do something," though who
she was addressing no one knew.

The Palomino ignored the cracking whip. He ran
straight for the two men waving sticks; he lengthened
his stride, took off and jumped over Joe with tremendous

60

cope; another second, and he was galloping away towards the mountains and freedom.

Mr. Miller slammed the field gate. "Well, of all the doggone horses . . . !" he exclaimed. "One can't help liking him though."

"I think he's heavenly," Mrs. Miller said.

Charlie and Joe were talking together. I dismounted and loosened Pelican's girths. Somehow, everything seemed flat.

"I don't believe we'll ever catch him," Wendy said.

"You were marvellous, Jean. I never knew the old horse had it in him," Mr. Miller told me, patting Pelican.

"No one can give him a bad name any more," Wendy said.

I could see Mrs. Miller laughing. "I don't know what you look like, Jean," she said.

"What about the rest of the cattle?" Pete asked.

"They'll be back in the mountains by now," Mr. Miller replied.

"Well, my mare's had more than enough," Phil said, patting the dun's neck.

"Poor old Sally's nearly all in. She was great, though," Wendy told me, kissing Sally's nose.

"Let's break off till after lunch anyway," Mr. Miller suggested. "I guess we've all had enough."

We took the horses back to the stable, and Joe appeared with Easter, and said, "The saddle's all broke up. And he's lost his bridle altogether."

I felt horribly guilty. I felt Pete looking at me.

"Never mind. Let's forget it," he said.

"I'm sorry. I'm really terribly sorry," I apologised. I didn't know what else to say. I couldn't offer to buy another one, because I hadn't any dollars.

"Don't worry, Jean. It doesn't matter at all. We've got dozens of saddles just rotting in the tack room," Wendy told me.

Phil was whistling a song called, "Don't let the Stars

He jumped over Joe with tremendous scope

et in your eyes." "If you never spoil another saddle, Jean, ou'll be doing all right," he said.

"There's the bridle too," I replied, taking off Pelican's ack.

"It was only an old one made up of scraps. He's got is own special show one. So do stop worrying, Jean," Wendy said.

We turned out the horses so that they could roll and cool off slowly.

"If we were posh, we'd slosh them down and get going with sweat scrapers. But it's too much trouble," Wendy told me.

We wandered indoors and ate large helpings of ice-cream from one of the refrigerators.

"You never caught the wild horse, then?" Annie asked, and then she started chasing Phil round the kitchen table, because he had spilt ice-cream on the floor. Mrs. Miller came in and said that we shouldn't be eating ice-cream just before lunch, and told us all to wash our hands and faces.

After we had tidied ourselves up, Wendy and I laid the dining-room table. There was cold rib roast, pineapple salad, corn, hot rolls and apple sauce for lunch. After we had finished eating, we caught the horses and gave them feeds. Peter and Phil disappeared to help with the harvest, and Wendy and I spent the afternoon playing with the dogs and looking at Wendy's books. We didn't have tea, but at five o'clock Phil and Pete returned and we all drank Cokes and ate chocolate, and bread and cheese, and some cookies which Annie had just made.

"A few more days and w'ell be through," Pete said, alluding to the harvest.

"And I shan't be sorry," Phil replied.

"I wish Daddy would let me drive one of the tractors. He knows I can," Wendy said.

"I'm going to fetch the rest of the cattle in now. Anyone like to help?" Pete asked.

"I'll open the gate for you when they're down off the

mountains," Phil replied. "But I'm darned if I'm doin
any more riding to-day."

"I'm going to read. I'm not half-way through the boo
Miss Saunders gave me to read during the vacation, an
school starts in another two or three weeks," Wend
replied.

In spite of the exciting morning I wasn't at all tirec
"I'd like to help," I said.

"That's fine. There's no one I would rather have," Pet
replied, looking at me seriously with his grey eyes.

"But who shall I ride? I'm sure Pelican's had enough,'
I said.

"You're welcome to my mare. She can go all day anc
she's still game at the end," Phil told me.

I thanked Phil, and then Pete and I collected tack fron
the saddle-room. The dun mare was very sweet. She
sniffed me all over and lowered her head, so that I coulc
put her bridle on. Pete gave me a leg up and then we se
off together across the valley.

Evening was in the air, and the mountains looked very
remote and blue in the gathering dusk. I admired the
landscape, and Pete said, "One day we must take you for
a moonlight ride. That's really something. You must
come cubbing soon, and later on foxhunting."

"That'll be lovely," I replied.

"I wish we could catch that darned horse this evening,"
Pete said. "I don't want to share him with Phil and Wendy,
because we'd be fighting all the time. But I wouldn't mind
going halves with you."

I felt stupidly embarrassed. I didn't like to explain that
I wanted the horse to be Angus's and mine and no one
else's. It would sound unfriendly, particularly when the
Millers had been so terribly kind to us. In the end I said
nothing, and we rode round the mountains in silence,
and then took a trail which I had never seen before.

I felt very high up on the dun mare. I think she was
the tallest horse I had ever ridden. She carried her head

rather too high and her stride was a bit short for a horse of nearly sixteen hands.

We collected cattle as we rode. Pete seemed an old hand at rounding up. Soon we had a herd of twelve or more and we turned for home, taking a trail which I knew. I told Pete how I wished to be a cowboy then and he laughed and told me about the jeeps and the cold winters out West. "Never mind, Jean, you can come and stay at my farm whenever you like and round up my cattle from dawn to dark," he said.

"That'll be super. Thank you very much," I replied. But I still wanted to live on a ranch with covered wagons, and long trips into the west, and camp fires. I shall just go on searching till I find a real ranch, I decided.

The sun was setting as we came to the valley. Behind the mountains the sky was red and gold. I felt like a character in a book or a film as I looked at our herd, and the dun's long neck and large ears, and the Millers' white house, with its windows lit up, with its pillars and the lake in front.

We should have lassoos, I thought, and revolvers in our holsters. We're not really dressed for the occasion. And our saddles were wrong too. Pete was whistling a tune I had never heard before. The dun mare walked with a swing. My life in England seemed far away and infinitely remote. Wendy and Phil were waiting by the field gate, whistling and talking, and chewing grass. They didn't seem so tall now that I knew them better, though I still felt tiny whenever I stood beside them.

"Looks as though you've got them all, Pete," Phil bawled.

The cattle weren't giving us much trouble, though they dodged a bit when they came to the gate. But presently, one of the calves separated from his mother and they both panicked. It took us nearly twenty minutes to get them together again.

It was quite dark when Pete and I rode round to the

65

C

stable-yard. The other horses had all been turned out.

"Did you enjoy it?" Pete asked.

"Yes, like anything. It was really super," I replied.

"I expect your brother will be okay to-morrow, and you'll be going back to Mountain Farm. We've really enjoyed having you. I just wanted to tell you that," Pete said, taking off his chestnut's saddle.

"It's been lovely. I've loved living here," I replied, and I realised suddenly how difficult to-morrow would be. I should have to face my parents, and they doubtless would be furious with the way Angus and I had behaved. I knew we had no excuse to offer; we had deliberately disobeyed every instruction they had given us, at least that's the way they would see it, and it would be mostly true. I didn't think we would be able to make them realise how completely we had lost our heads when we had seen the Palomino and the bay mare. They'd never understand, and anyway it was inexcusable not to turn back later when we had remembered. I expect we won't be allowed to ride for ages and ages, I thought gloomily, and I saw us hanging around Mountain Farm day after day with absolutely nothing to do.

We fed the horses and put the tack away. "It's been a lovely day. I've enjoyed every moment of it. It's really been one of the loveliest days I've ever spent," I told Pete, as we walked up to the house together.

"I've enjoyed it too," he said.

Supper was waiting for us. The dining-room table was lit by candle-light. We ate fresh water fish cooked in wine, asparagus, hot rolls and peaches and ice-cream. I felt quite sick, when eventually I stopped eating.

"Your father rang up. He'll be fetching you before he goes to Washington in the morning," Mr. Miller told me.

"Right. I'll be ready. How's Angus?" I asked.

"Fine. Full of life." Mr. Miller replied. "There's not a scratch on him."

After supper we all helped wash up; then Pete and I

wandered down to the stable and turned out the two horses we had ridden.

Wendy and I went to bed soon after that. The night was terribly warm and I didn't sleep for hours. The moon rose round and red and shone on our two beds; the frogs sang incessantly; rooks cawed raucously and circled the large trees beyond the lawn. I thought of Angus in the hospital, of Mountain Farm empty dreaming in the moonlight, of the friends I had left behind in England. I hoped that Moonlight and Mermaid were happy, and then, at last, I slept.

CHAPTER SEVEN

I GOT UP very early. I wanted to say good-bye to all the animals, before I left. I had an idea it would be ages before I was allowed to see the Millers' house again.

Charlie and Joe were milking the house cows. They asked after Angus and let me try my hand at it. They were very pleased that Angus wasn't hurt. They told me that they each had the milk from one cow as part of their wage, as well as a house, flour and firewood. I wasn't much good at milking.

The horses were waiting at their field gate. They were very friendly, and the dun mare whinnied when she saw me. The dogs appeared and Cop licked my face, and Susie brought me a stick to throw. It was a lovely morning with a light mist on the mountains. I knew it would be very hot later. I looked at the cattle, already restless because of the flies. They were all mixed up still, but I knew that later they would be separated, some to go back to the mountains, some to be killed for meat, and some to stay in the fields. I wandered back to the house and met Pete. "You get earlier and earlier," he said.

We fed the horses together, and Pete asked whether I

would like to take Easter and the bay mare back to Mountain Farm. I said that I'd better ask my parents first.

I hate departures—except from places like school—and this seemed a particularly bad one, though I was only going to the other side of the valley.

I hardly ate any breakfast. When I had finished I said good-bye to Annie, and then I heard Daddy hooting impatiently outside the front door. I rushed into the dining-room, where the Millers were still eating and shrieked good-bye to everyone. I kissed Cop, and rushing oustide I ran straight into a pillar.

Daddy said, "Do look where you're going. Have you hurt yourself? We don't want any more accidents."

I rubbed my head, and said, "No, thank you."

I hit my head again as I got into the car. "You seem determined to do yourself in," Daddy remarked.

I felt cross. "How's Angus?" I asked.

"Completely recovered," Daddy replied.

I waited for him to ask how we came to be in the mountains. But he didn't. We drove away from the Millers' house, along the long drive, in silence.

Mountain Farm looked very small. The yard seemed tiny. Daddy said, "I'll just drop you and drive on. I'm late already.

Angus was waiting by the front door. "Hallo," he shrieked.

He looked marvellous, but tiny after Phil and Pete. "I only had concussion," he said. "The hospital was awful; they kept me in a darkened room; and there was absolutely nothing to do."

"Hallo, Jean," Mummy said, appearing from the house. "Did you have a nice time?"

"Super. The Millers were all terribly kind," I replied.

I felt as though I had been away a very long time.

"Did you have an awful time?" I asked Mummy.

"Yes, at the beginning; though we found quite a nice

little hotel. It was better when we knew what was wrong with Angus," she replied.

Angus and I wandered round to the stable. "You know we're not to ride again for the whole holidays, don't you?" he asked.

I felt a huge lump rising in my throat.

"I told them everything. What else could I do?" he asked.

"Of course. You couldn't do anything else," I said.

"It sounded so awful when I started to explain. Not at all like it really was. I expect you could have told them better," Angus said. "They were jolly nice about it really. I mean I suppose we had to have some sort of punishment really. I expect if we had children, we'd do just the same."

"You mean about punishing them?" I asked. "Personally, I'd much rather be smacked, or made to write *I must do what my parents tell me,* five hundred times. Wouldn't you?"

"Much. But the point is they wanted to choose the worst punishment they could think of ," Angus said.

"Well, they've certainly succeeded," I replied. I saw the rest of the holidays stretching before us, long sunny days, beautiful early mornings. I saw the mountains calling us, their trails waiting to be explored. And we'll be stuck here, I thought, with no horses to ride. We'll see the Millers riding past, horses grazing in the valley, and we'll know that till term starts we can't ride anywhere, not even to the end of the dirt road and back. "We'll never catch the wild horse now," I said.

"Well, it's our own fault. We can't blame anyone else. It's no good being cross. We'll just have to make the best of it," Angus replied.

"I suppose we can walk where we like?" I asked.

"Not off the property for a week," Angus replied.

"We may as well commit suicide," I said.

"Don't be so hysterical. What's a week or a month? A mere drop in the ocean of our lives," Angus replied.

I could see that my brother had been considering our punishment for some time and was now determined to make the best of it. I started to tell him about my stay with the Millers.

"They were all really terribly nice; though I think I like Pete best," I finished.

"What did you do with the chocolates?" Angus asked.

"Ate them of course. I've still got the pen though," I replied.

"You might have kept some for your poor sick brother," Angus said.

"I decided that you probably had piles of grapes and peaches. Sick people always get masses to eat," I replied.

We wandered into the house and out again. There seemed absolutely nothing to do. Mummy told us to tidy our bedrooms, which she said were like pigsties. I began to dread the next week.

"We'll have to write poetry or something," Angus said.

After lunch Pete rang up. He wanted to know whether we'd like some horses brought over. I explained about our punishment, and he said, "Tough luck. Never mind, if you can't come to us, we'll come to you. We've got two-thirds of the harvest in. There's nothing to stop us bringing sandwiches and spending the whole darned day with you. So cheer up, we'll come right over to-morrow, Jean."

I said, "Gosh! That'll be super. But remember we can't ride. What will you do all day?"

"Plenty. I've got all sorts of ideas," Pete replied. "Be seeing you."

I told Angus what Pete had said. He looked worried. "I can't see what the heck they'll do here all day," he said. "They're not the sort of people who can sit about and read for hours."

"Well, it's no good worrying. I've told them how the land lies," I replied.

We spent the afternoon reading books. We told Mummy about the Millers' impending visit, and she said:

"I can't imagine what they'll do all day. I should think they'd be bored to tears."

The paddock and the stable looked horribly empty without any horses. The evening dragged slowly on till bed-time.

I wakened the next morning filled with trepidation. I was certain Mummy was right—the Millers would be bored to tears.

I saw them yawning and looking at their watches. I wished that they hadn't decided to come. Angus felt the same. We both appeared for breakfast with dismal faces.

It was another perfect day. "If only we had a swimming pool," Angus said.

"Or a tennis court, or even a swing," I added.

"I'm glad you haven't either. You're dangerous enough as it is," Mummy said.

"I can't see that there's anything dangerous in a swing," Angus replied.

"Can't you? Read a few Victorian children's books and you'll soon see there is," Mummy answered. "For one thing, you'd probably knock each other's eyes out with the corners, or go so high that you'd become entangled with a tree."

I was furious that Mummy could think we'd be so silly. I'd often played with swings before. It was maddening not to be trusted at all. One day we'll show Mummy and Daddy what we're really like, I thought.

The Millers arrived in the jeep at ten o'clock. Phil was driving. Apparently, you can have a licence at fifteen in most States as long as your parents agree.

"We've brought some white-wash. We thought we'd start on the inside of the stable," Wendy yelled.

"What a super idea," Angus said.

Phil drove the jeep into the yard and we all helped pull out white-wash buckets and brushes.

"We wanted to bring the men along to help some. But the old man wasn't agreeable," Pete told us.

"I'm starting on the cobwebs. Do you think you could

get the cobweb brush out of the kitchen for me, Angus?"
Wendy asked.

"I expect we'll have to brush down the walls first,"
Pete said.

We spent the entire morning white-washing the stable.
It looked marvellous by lunch time. Wendy broke the
cobweb brush, and insisted on going indoors to apologise
to Mummy. Phil cracked jokes all the time and was
terribly gay. The Millers wouldn't come in for lunch.
They said they'd only upset our parents, and anyway they
weren't suitably dressed.

After lunch, Wendy suggested that we should play some
sort of hiding game, and Angus suggested hide and seek.
The Millers had never heard of it, and I explained the
rules, and then we began. Angus and I were the first
He's. Home was the back door. We counted fifty in the
kitchen and then we started to search. I found Phil quite
quickly, but of course I couldn't catch him, because he
ran much too fast. Angus found Wendy, but exactly the
same thing happened to him—she ran madly to the back
door, leaving him miles behind. Pete slunk home while
neither of us was looking: so we were still He's. It
wasn't until our third attempt that we managed to catch
anyone and then I caught Pete in the garage. So now he
and Angus were He's. I had made up my mind some time
ago as to where I would hide. I hurried down to one
of the lower corners of the paddock, where there are
brambles, a small ditch and boulders, and there I hid.
I knew that I was wonderfully concealed, as I settled
myself comfortably half in the ditch and half on a
boulder. I was in the shade and there was a lovely smell
of wet earth. The paddock wall was on three sides of
me. I didn't think anyone wouldd find me for hours.
There was green stuff growing by the ditch which had a
peculiar smell, which reminded me of some plant in
England; but which particular one I couldn't determine.

I listened to Pete chasing Wendy down by the house
and heard her triumphant yell of "Home." I heard Phil

laughing; then ages seemed to pass before someone said, "She must be in the paddock." I thought of all the times I had played hide-and-seek at home in England. I remembered how I had dreaded the Millers coming, and realised how wrong I had been. And then, I heard a rustling noise quite close. Something was coming towards me through the brambles. I tried to keep calm, but already I was afraid. I imagined a rat or a ground hog. I was horribly cornered. I'm not generally nervous—I suppose some animal instinct warned me of danger. For the first time in my life I wanted to scream. And then I heard a hiss, and then I did scream; for coming towards me was a snake with beady eyes, and a poisonous tongue and a long slippery body. The wall was behind me and the ditch. There was no escape. The snake was thrashing in the undergrowth, his whole appearance belonged to a killer. I screamed and screamed again. I heard yells in the stable-yard. I backed into the ditch and searched frantically for a boulder I could throw. They were all enormous, and now I was right against the wall. It seemed to me that my last hour had come. I tore off one of my shoes and hurled it at the snake's hideous head. But it only made him angrier. He thrashed the ground madly with his body and hissed ferociously; he seemed to spit at me, and his eyes glistened with evil intent.

I cried, "Help, help!" but now I was almost paralysed with fear.

And then I heard people coming. "Where are you?" Angus cried. He sounded a long way behind the others.

"In the corner by the wall. It's a snake," I yelled.

I pulled off my other shoe and hit the snake across the head, and leapt sideways just in time to miss his lunging head. I didn't notice the mud in the ditch in spite of my bare feet.

Phil arrived first. With one quick movement he threw a boulder which hit the snake in the middle.

"Jump for it, Jean," he cried.

I sprang to safety as the snake turned to face Phil. I

felt completely limp and my heart was pounding like an express train.

Wendy arrived. "Pete's gone back for a bar, or something," she said.

"He's a real killer. I was only just in time," Phil told us

We backed away from the snake, and then Angus arrived.

It seemed to me that my last hour had come

"Gosh, I thought you were being murdered, Jean," he exclaimed.

"She was very nearly," Phil replied.

Pete appeared with a long plank and a shovel. "It's all I can find. If we can't kill him with that, it's just our tough luck. Are you all right, Jean?" he asked.

"She's lost one of her shoes," Phil said. The snake had

disappeared in the undergrowth. Phil nudged him out with the plank.

"We'll kill you if it's the last thing we do," Pete said, gazing furiously at the snake.

I moved back farther. I hate seeing animals killed.

"Can't we leave him alone now?" I asked.

"And let him do the same thing to someone else?" Phil replied. And now a battle began. Phil and Pete beat the snake with the board and shovel. He was too quick and clever to let them hit him on the head. But gradually they paralysed his back half, until at last he could only lunge furiously with his gruesome face and a few inches of neck. Finally, Pete caught him a sideways blow and, quite suddenly, he lay still. I started to walk away then; I felt sick, whether because I had been so frightened or because the killing of the snake had filled me with disgust, I'm not sure. I could hear the others prodding the snake and discussing him in excited voices. I took off my other shoe and hurried towards the house barefoot.

Mummy was in the kitchen making tea. I helped her lay the table and then I told her about the snake and how I had only just escaped. She was terribly upset. Like Angus and I, she hadn't realised there were snakes in Virginia.

"You must never go near them again," she said. "Nor must Angus."

The others came in and we all had a lovely English tea in the kitchen. The Millers were full of my adventure. Pete had retrieved my missing shoe. They terrified Mummy more and more, until, at last, she said that if they didn't stop talking about the snake, she'd never let Angus and me out of her sight again. Such a suggestion was so awful that everyone changed the subject immediately and no one mentioned the snake again during tea.

We discussed the stable for a bit and decided that the doors should be painted dark green. Then Pete said:

"Did you realise that you were sitting in a bed of ground ivy down by the ditch, Jean?"

"No, I don't know what ground ivy looks like. What wrong with it, anyway?" I asked.

"You'll know soon," Phil replied, and he started t laugh.

"You'll be itching like mad soon, and you'll come u in a darned awful rash. That's what ground ivy does t you," Wendy explained.

It seemed that I still had a great deal to learn. "I see," I said, and started to itch immediately.

"That's just the power of suggestion," Mummy said as I began to scratch.

"It won't be soon. Poor Jean! It's been a darned awful day for you," Phil told me.

"We don't seem very lucky," Angus said.

We all washed up and then we wandered outside and discussed the snake all over again. Phil explained how some snakes are killers and some quite harmless. He told us how to tell the difference; but I didn't seem able to concentrate, and I can't remember any of the conversation now.

My arms were red and patchy and my legs and feet itched ceaselessly. I had a headache too. Altogether, I felt fairly miserable.

The Millers left quite soon, because they had to return the jeep by six o'clock, when the men would need it to take them home. I thanked them all for rescuing me, before they drove away. They said silly things like "Darned generous of us," and "Can't think why we did."

Angus and I watched the jeep disappearing along the dirt road. "You can't say to-day's been dull," Angus said.

"Far from it," I agreed.

CHAPTER EIGHT

THE NEXT few days were terribly dull. I wrote some very bad poetry; Angus made two saddle-racks to hang in the stable. Mummy bought us a pot of paint and we painted the loose-box doors dark green. We spent one ghastly afternoon visiting our new school. Mr. Miller came with us and our parents, and introduced us to the headmaster. It was a school for boys as well as girls; Pete and Phil had just left for a Military Academy; Wendy would be leaving after Christmas. There was a baseball pitch, and the buildings were low, modern and rambling. The headmaster, Mr. Beeton, was tall with narrow shoulders and fair hair. He gave us all tea in his small, two-storey, brick house. He was not at all frightening, and talked to Angus and me as though we were grown-ups. We discovered that our education was in advance of American children of our age. Mummy and Daddy seemed well pleased with the school, and Mr. Beeton. And we thought it very nice of him to give us tea, which is not a usual American meal.

On Sunday we all went to church. The service was quite short. Phil, Pete and Wendy sang in the choir. Mr. and Mrs. Miller were very smart with elegant hats and gloves.

The next day, Wendy, Pete and Phil turned up at Mountain Farm again with the jeep stacked high with wood.

"Hiya," they called when they saw us. "We thought we might build a corral to catch that darned horse in, and what better place could we think of than your back yard?"

"That is, if you don't mind," Pete said.

"Not at all," Angus replied.

I thought of Daddy and wondered whether he would

77

object; but I didn't say anything, because I was so pleased to see the Millers again and I was delighted by the thought of a corral in our own back yard.

The Millers had brought enormous posts and rails.

"Luckily the men have just started cutting the scrub back from the mountains; so there's plenty of wood back home," Wendy explained.

First we dug holes for the posts. The ground was very hard, but the Millers seemed tireless. They had brought a few bottles of beer in the jeep and we refreshed ourselves at intervals. I was glad that Daddy was in Washington, because I didn't think he would approve of the beer. Fortunately, Mummy was madly making curtains in the dining-room.

"We must make the rails at least ten feet high. We can't risk losing him once we've got him here," Pete said, alluding to the wild horse.

"We'll make the corral I guess about fifteen by twenty; then he can exercise himself a bit; because he'll have to stay here till he's tame," Phil told us.

We had the posts up at last. "We'd better have slip rails for the entrance, hadn't we?" Angus asked.

"Yeah, with padlocks, I guess. We can't afford to have him stolen," Phil replied.

The Millers were rather organising. I could see that they ruffled Angus. They didn't seem to think that we were capable of arranging anything, and the yard might have been theirs, for all the notice they took of our suggestions. After a bit I disappeared to help Mummy get lunch. She wasn't very pleased about the corral. "Don't you think you should ask Daddy, before you start knocking in posts?" she asked. "It may be the Millers' farm, but Daddy's paying rent for it."

"It's a bit late. It's half-built already," I replied.

"Well, don't blame me, if he makes you pull it all down," Mummy said.

I didn't say anything. I was horribly worried. I couldn't imagine what the Millers would say if we had to pull down the corral five minutes after it was built. It might make us enemies for life.

"I hope they're staying for lunch?" Mummy said.

"I expect so," I replied.

I made a large salad and Mummy opened a tin of tongue. We boiled some potatoes and made an apple Charlotte. Then I wandered outside to see how the work was progressing.

The corral overshadowed the whole yard. It was three-quarters built. I had meant to tell the Millers just what Mummy had said about Daddy objecting, and ordering it to be pulled down. But somehow I couldn't bear to. Everyone was laughing and singing as they sawed and hammered; and anyway, it was a bit late, since the corral was almost finished. Instead I said:

"You'll stay to lunch, won't you?"

"Sure, we'd love to," Phil replied with a grin.

"We're rather a crowd," Pete said.

"That doesn't make any difference at all," I answered.

"Can I call up Mummy and let her know? We don't want to make her mad," Wendy said.

"Of course," I replied.

I took Wendy indoors and she rang up her mother. Then we helped Mummy lay the table for lunch. Later we discussed school as we ate.

"You know you'll have to call the teachers Sir and Ma'am, don't you?" Phil asked.

"No, I didn't actually," I replied

"Virginian children call their parents Sir and Ma'am, and their parents' friends," Pete told us.

"We always rag Mr. Beeton. We call him Sunny Boy," Wendy said, and told us all about the masters and mistresses, how they differed and which you could cheek and which you couldn't. I think Mummy was bored. It seemed to me that American children could get away with quite a lot in school.

We finished the corral after lunch. We were all rather proud of it.

"We'll have a shot at getting the wild horse to-morrow. It's a real shame you can't ride. You'll just have to stand around and be ready to put the rails up when he's in,' Phil said, and I looked at Angus and he looked away at the mountains. I felt that we were paying dearly for the day our parents spent in Washington.

"It's too bad. I'm really sorry," Pete said, and he sounded it.

"Your parents are real strict. I thought they'd have relented by now," Wendy told us.

I hate being pitied, and I hate anyone criticising Mummy and Daddy.

"It doesn't matter. It's our own fault," I replied, also looking at the mountains, blue and gold and still beneath the midday sun.

"Well, I think it's a real shame," Pete said.

"Look out for us to-morrow about nine, will you?" Phil asked. "We'll make an early start. One of the men saw the darned horse quite near with a couple of Hodge's mares yesterday. Everyone's beginning to get really mad with him. Hodge's says he'll shoot at sight."

"Not really? How awful," I said, and I saw the Palomino lying still, his lovely golden coat soaked in blood; his eyes staring, not seeing.

"No one wants him alive any more. They say he'll never be any use now," Wendy told us.

"They think he's nuts," Pete said.

"More fools them," Angus replied.

The Millers drove away. I told Angus what Mummy and said about Daddy and the corral, and he said why hadn't I told him before. Then we had one of those tiresome, pointless quarrels, which always occur when we're both dreading something and are tired. The thing we were dreading was, of course, Daddy's return; and, even more, the possibility of having to pull down the corral, and the Millers' reaction.

We argued and argued and then we heard a car coming along the dirt road and knew it was Daddy. I had an awful impulse to hide and leave Angus to deal with the situation, but I controlled myself. There was hardly enough room left for Daddy to put the car in the garage.

"I bet we've done the wrong thing again. Why are we so hopeless?" I asked Angus.

Daddy shut the garage doors. "What on earth's all this?" he called.

"It's a corral," Angus replied.

"I hope you don't mind. It's for the wild horse," I told him with a rush.

"It doesn't make the yard look very pretty does it? Can't you kids think of anything but that wretched horse?" Daddy asked, and he didn't sound cross at all.

I felt like cheering. "No, not really," I replied. "I'm sorry we didn't ask you before we put it up."

Daddy examined the corral. "You've really made quite a good job of it. I suppose the Millers helped?" he said.

We told him how the Millers had come and spent all day and he told us that we were crazy to keep chasing the wild horse.

"Why don't you try taming him for a change?" he suggested.

"It's certainly an idea," I said.

"If we can ever get within a hundred yards of him," added Angus.

Daddy had bought an already cooked chicken on his way home and we had an enormous supper. We were all very gay and we laughed a great deal about the wild horse and the corral.

Daddy said that we were becoming horse maniacs, and Mummy said she couldn't imagine what we would do with the Palomino once we caught him, since, by all accounts, he was unrideable. Angus said, "*Nothing venture, nothing win. He who never makes mistakes never makes anything*," which I had quoted to him since hearing it from Wendy.

Angus and I wakened early the next morning and at nine o'clock we started watching for the Millers.

"I suppose if they do drive the wild horse in here, he'll be theirs," I said, looking at the corral.

"I suppose so," Angus replied, a trifle dismally.

It was a hazy morning. The sort of morning which makes you think of cub-hunting and an English lane woven with cobwebs. Or of mushrooms and dewy black-berries. I remember that I felt very far from home as we waited by the corral. I think Angus did too, because he suddenly said, "I wish it would rain occasionally. To-day would be perfect if only there was a faint drizzle."

I laughed, because in England Angus always grumbled about the rain. "It's a pity you missed the thunderstorm," I replied.

We couldn't see the mountains at all; only our paddock and a little of the hill beyond were visible.

"I wish they'd come," Angus said. "We both hate waiting.

"They may be hours," I replied.

We collected windfall peaches from the lawn and ate them.

"Do you know they still plough with oxen in Georgia and the deep South? Pete told me," Angus said.

"It's quite different from what we expected. Do you think we've changed a lot?" I asked.

"Quite a bit. I think we're wilder than we used to be," Angus replied seriously.

"We've learnt several things. I mean we can manage a washing machine, a washing-up machine and an electric cooker now," I said.

"Touch wood," Angus replied.

Time passed very slowly. We collected apples from the apple tree and drank some lime juice. Angus began to grumble.

"I don't believe they're ever coming. Why should we wait about all day for them? It's not as though the horse will be ours if they do catch it. It's not in our interest to wait."

I was shocked, though Angus was only putting my own thoughts into words. "How can you be so selfish? After all the Millers have done for us . . ." I cried.

"What bosh. What have they done?" Angus asked.

"Lent us horses, stocked our larder with food, been nice when we lost their horses. No one could have been nicer to us," I replied.

"Well, here they come," Angus said.

Hoofs were coming over the hill, lots of hoofs. I wanted to run and wave; instead I said, "We'd better move out of the way. We don't want the Palomino to see us."

"If they've got him," Angus replied.

I wondered why my brother was so disparaging. Later, I was to realise that he was jealous of Pete and Phil, who had horses and cars to drive, and dogs and lots of pocket money, while we had no horse of our own, no driving licences, no dogs and very little pocket money. But I didn't know that then.

"I think you're absolutely beastly," I cried. "Why must you run down the Millers the whole time? I like them."

"I've noticed that," Angus answered.

We each stood on one side of the corral in disagreeable silence. The Millers came over the hill like cavalry and in front of them was the wild horse. I did cheer then. I shouted, "Hurray, hurray, they've got him."

Then I remembered that once he was in the corral he would never be ours, and I didn't know what to think; because I liked the Millers, and I wanted them to have him; but if they did, I knew that we would never have a horse of our own. It was a fearful dilemma, and now they were coming down the hill. The Palomino looked wonderful, like the star horse in a Wild West film, only more phantom and more beautiful. Phil was quite close.

Pete was riding to the left of the Palomino. Wendy was a long way behind.

"Spread out. Jean. We'll see to the rails," Phil shouted.

Angus and I took up new positions in the paddock. My heart was beating madly with excitement. There was so much at stake. I still didn't know what I hoped would happen. And there wasn't time to think any more. Phil was hustling the wild horse. I guessed that he didn't want him to see the corral and know the fate which awaited him.

The Palomino wheeled

The Palomino came quite close to me. I could see the steam rising from him and the fear that showed in his eyes. I remembered what Daddy had said—"Why don't you try and tame him?"—Would he ever be tame? I wondered.

Angus was waving his arms. I heard Mummy slam the back door. I could hear the frogs' chorus in the low land. They'll catch him, I thought, they'll tame him and ride him, and Angus and I will know that our dream has died, that there's no hope any more. The Palomino was galloping straight toward the corral. It's all over now—he's there, I told myself, and I was furious that I felt no thrill. I must be terribly selfish, I decided.

The Palomino saw the corral. but too late. Angus and I started to run as he galloped into it with Phil on his tail. "Hurry," yelled Pete.

I had expected Phil to put up the rails, but he couldn't stop in time. The Palomino wheeled on his hocks; Phil leapt to the ground; Angus and I ran still faster; Pete yelled. But we were all too late. With a flourish of his head, the Palomino looked at us all for one split second, then he was out of the corral, dodging Pete and suddenly lost again in the mist and the peace of the valley.

Phil said a whole lot of words Angus and I are never allowed to use. Then everyone started blaming everyone else. It was a horrible moment and the awful thing was I wasn't really sorry. The Millers became very angry, and then suddenly they agreed that it really wasn't anybody's fault, but just bad luck and too little forethought. I have never ceased to marvel at the way American children can abuse each other hideously, using the worst possible insults, and a few minutes later have made it all up. Within five minutes of the Palomino's disappearance. everyone was laughing and happy, making plans for a fresh attempt.

CHAPTER NINE

BEFORE PETE and Phil left for school they brought back the bay mare and Frances to Mountain Farm. We were all very sad now that the summer holidays were over. We hadn't caught the wild horse and Daddy had made us take down the corral as he didn't want it to become a permanent fixture. The weather was still marvellous; the mountains had become a mass of greens, browns and oranges; there was a feeling of autumn in the air or what the Millers called the 'fall.'

Daddy was much busier. Often he didn't return from Washington except for week-ends. Our previous life in England seemed very far away. Wendy gave us one of her cat's kittens. He was tiny and grey with a white waistcoat. We called him Cassius, and Cassy for short.

Phil and Pete said good-bye on a misty morning. They looked very dashing in their military type school uniform. They wore white pipeclayed belts, and every buckle and every button on their tunics was shining.

We stood together in the yard and Phil said, "It's not long before we'll be back again. and then we really will catch that darned horse."

"If you haven't caught him already." Pete added.

"You'll be pretty smart if you do," Phil said, using smart in the American sense when it means clever, cunning or sharp, or really a mixture of all three.

"I don't think we will," Wendy replied.

"We're jolly well going to try, anyway," Angus said.

Pete kicked a stone and we stood and said nothing, while the mist cleared from the mountains and the sun shone on the valley.

"I hope you get on all right at school, Jean. I guess
86

you may find it kind of rough after life in England," Pete told me.

"I'll look after her all right," Wendy said.

"She's champion wrestler in the school and Captain of the baseball team," Phil told us.

Pete and Phil left at last and when they had gone the holidays seemed really over. Angus and I stood and talked to the horses. It was lovely to have them back again. but it seemed a bit late now that term was just about to start. Wendy had gone home. The yard seemed very quiet. The remains of the corral lay by the stable wall.

"I hate departures," exclaimed Angus:

"I'm dreading to-morrow," I replied. "I wonder if one's expected to behave like a new girl in an American school."

"It sounds as though one has to fight tooth and claw." Angus said.

To-morrow was to be our first day at school in America. I think we both dreaded it, though we were filled with a great curiosity. Mummy had ordered our school uniforms from Washington. I hated my grey tunic and white blouse With it I was to wear white ankle socks and leather moccasins.

"Wendy says we get home at about half-past four in the evening, which doesn't sound too bad," Angus said.

"But there's loads of 'prep,' and I expect it will all seem awfully difficult at first," I replied pessimistically.

"I don't see why. We've done a year's French already and our form's only just beginning. It should be awfully easy for us," Angus said.

"What about American history and current affairs?" I asked.

"Oh, we'll soon pick that up. Anyway, with any luck, they'll be doing English history this term," Angus answered cheerfully.

We couldn't ride till term started. We spent the afternoon thinking about school and helping Mummy tidy

up the house. The day passed very slowly. Mr. Mille.
was to collect us next morning in the Buick. It seemed
peculiar to have nothing to prepare or pack. I made some
cakes; Angus read *A Short History of America*, which he
found in the sitting-room.

Mummy made us go to bed early and I didn't sleep for
hours. We had left Frances and the bay mare in for fear
the wild horse might appear again and entice them away
I could hear them moving about in their boxes and
munching hay as I tried to sleep. I counted sheep and did
algebra in my head. I recited French verbs and Latin
declensions. I drew a map of Europe in my head, and
thought about politics. Still I couldn't sleep. I crept into
my parents' room and took some aspirins. Outside a
new moon glistened in a dark sky. Stars hung sparkling
in the stillness of night. A searchlight shone over the
mountains, its soft beam moving backwards and forwards.
watching for planes to guide on their way. There wasn't
even a breeze; only the frogs broke the silence of
the valley. The aspirins worked, I fell asleep to dream
that Daddy was teaching us American history in the
kitchen.

I passed my first day at our new school in a sort of
daze. Nobody seemed to do much work; Wendy chaper-
oned me from one lesson to another. I learned how to
hold a baseball bat and not to mind when people laughed
at my English accent. Angus had a fight with a boy
called Bobby and held his own. No one seemed to treat
the teachers with great respect. We weren't given 'prep'
to take home because it was our first day. In the evening
we rode. The bay mare was very fresh and Angus fell off.
We didn't tell Mummy.

Angus, Wendy and I made great plans for the week-end.
We were all determined to catch the wild horse before
term ended. We arranged to take a sandwich lunch on
Saturday and ride far into the mountains. Angus and I
rode Frances and the bay mare every evening and mucked
out their boxes before we left for school in the morning.

Daddy had forbidden us to go far without Wendy, little knowing how recklessly she behaved on occasions.

Saturday dawned fair and warm. Angus and I breakfasted at an early hour by ourselves in the kitchen. We mucked out the loose-boxes, wishing that the floors were of concrete instead of beaten earth. We groomed the ponies and I washed Frances's quarters and tail which were very dirty.

Wendy arrived at half-past eight riding Pete's chestnut. "I should put on plenty. It'll be cold where we're going," she told us.

The valley was full of cattle. Wendy had brought Cop and Susie. "They won't be any trouble: rabies is just over now in the mountains," she said.

We cantered steadily across the valley. We followed a trail rust, green, orange, yellow red and brown. Above the sky was blue; the sun shone, birds sang. We were riding in the Blue Ridge Mountains of Virginia in the famous American fall, and our surroundings were indescribably beautiful. Frances puffed rather; Angus and Wendy rode ahead chattering about wars long past. I remembered England in the autumn, cottages on a green, leaves falling silently on leaves. the changing colour of the hedges, fires in dusty grates. The beauty of America was vaster, more overpowering. more sensational, I decided. One felt less of an individual; one could die on a mountain trail and the crows would pick your bones and the cattle would look at you with their large liquid eyes and months later someone would stumble over your remains. England was smaller and kinder and less breathtaking. I decided, hurrying Frances, whose walk was becoming a crawl.

We left the trail and reached the gas line. We cantered and turned left when we came to a sandy road. Cop and Susie were still with us.

"We must watch for hoof marks soon. He was seen around here a couple of days ago," Wendy said, alluding to the wild horse.

"What are our plans?" I asked.

"To follow him until he's cornered." Wendy replied.

"But that might be for ever," I answered.

"There's nothing else we can do. Do be sensible, Jean, Angus said.

"We could try to make friends with him," I replied.

"Oh sure. What about him galloping off?" Wend asked.

"He might not, if we didn't chase him," I replied Angus and Wendy laughed.

"What a hope," Angus said.

I could see that Wendy and Angus were determined to stand by one another. "We're just making him wilder and wilder," I complained. "No one will ever be able to catch him soon, and he'll end up by getting shot."

"Phooey," Wendy replied.

I was suddenly furious. I was angry with Angus for backing up Wendy. Apparently he had forgotten that blood is thicker than water, and I was infuriated by Wendy's 'Phooey.'

"Well, I'm not chasing him anyway," I exclaimed. "I think it's half-witted and jolly silly."

"Okay, now we know." Angus replied.

I think I must have been in a terribly bad temper; because a moment later when I saw hoofprints which didn't belong to any of our horses I said nothing. I watched the hoofprints as I rode on and, when I saw they turned down a trail on our right, I followed them without saying a word to Angus and Wendy.

The trail I took was narrow, well worn and partly concealed by clumps of rocks; often it nearly petered out altogether. It was more suitable for someone on foot than a horse. I felt very happy to be alone and I was sure that Wendy and Angus deserved the fright they would get when they discovered that I had disappeared. Frances wasn't so pleased; she shied frequently and tried to turn back. Once she neighed, and I was surprised by an answering neigh from farther along the track. I think

hat's when I first started to feel excited. I had imagined
he wild horse several miles away, but the answering
eigh sounded quite near. Of course, it could belong to
completely strange horse; but I didn't think that very
kely as I hurried Frances along the trail.

Presently, I thought I heard a holler. It might have
een Angus calling, but I didn't dare reply. because of
rightening the wild horse. They'll retrace their steps and
ee Frances's hoofprints, I thought, imagining Angus and
Wendy turning their horses. Then I saw smoke ahead. a
hin thread disappearing among the tree tops towards the
blue sky. I didn't know what to expect after that. I
orgot Wendy and Angus altogether. I couldn't canter because of the frequent boulders, but I pushed Frances
into a fast trot and suddenly we turned a corner and
there in front was a wooden building. My heart stood
still, not because of the building and an old man cutting
grass, but because tied to a stake stood the Palomino.
Frances had stopped dead when she saw what was ahead
of us. The Palomino whinnied and the old man looked
up. I didn't feel excited any more. Only sick with disappointment. I had never imagined a stranger catching
the Palomino. Quite suddenly my dreams had fallen to
the ground in one appalling crash. The man continued
his grass cutting. I saw that the building stood in a tiny.
well-concealed clearing and that beyond there was only
a forest of trees growing from among boulders. Frances
was longing to retreat in spite of the appealing glances
from the Palomino. I didn't know what to do. At last, I
rode forward into the clearing.

The Palomino looked much smaller tied to a stake. He
whinnied again and Frances answered. I saw that the
man cutting grass wasn't so old and that he carried a
revolver in his belt. He hadn't shaved for several days
and he looked like a ruffian in an old-fashioned illustra-
tion from *The Babes in the Wood*. I think I started to
feel scared then. Frances was scared too. She moved forward cautiously, every nerve tense.

Tied to a stake stood the Palomino

"And what do you want?" the man asked. suddenly turning round.

I hadn't thought of anything to say. Frances had halted. I sat stupidly silent.

"How clever of you to catch the wild horse." I said at last, simply to gain time.

The man didn't seem to hear me.

"You beat it. Do you hear me? Get out of here real fast or you'll be sorry," he said, and his voice was menacing.

My first impulse was to do just as he said. But a sense of pride and the sight of the Palomino tethered to a stake stopped me.

"I wondered whether you would sell him," I replied, pointing at the wild horse.

"Not to you. Now beat it." the man answered. But I didn't intend being defeated so easily.

"I'm thirsty. Can I have some water?" I asked.

"Ride back along the trail and you'll see a spring," the man replied. "It's God's water. You can do no better."

"I didn't see it coming along. May I speak to your horse?" I asked, dismounting and approaching the Palomino.

I knew that I was being infuriating. But I wanted to find out more about the man and why he lived alone in the mountains. He didn't look like a hermit. He didn't really look like a gangster. But I guessed that somehow he was outside the law. Most of all I wanted to strike a bargain with him over the wild horse.

The Palomino snorted as I approached.

"Watch it. I don't want him loose," the man said. I put out a hand and patted the Palomino's golden neck. He stiffened as I touched him and watched me apprehensively. I could feel the man watching me too. His eyes seemed to bore through my back. Frances and the Palomino touched noses and then I heard a commotion behind us. I turned and saw that the man held his revolver in one hand. He was ready to shoot, and coming along the trail were Wendy and Angus. "Don't fire," cried.

"Hi," yelled Wendy. "What the heck are you doing?" She hadn't seen the man.

"Careful," I cried. "There's a man here with a gun."

"What? We can't hear a word you're saying," yelled Angus.

"They're friends of mine. Please don't shoot." I said to the man.

He put away his gun. "They're only kids, are they? I thought they were the cops," he said.

Wendy and Angus entered the clearing and I rushed forward and explained the situation to them.

"He's old Rob, the moonshiner," Wendy said, when I had finished. "The sheriff's looking for him; that's why he's so scared."

"What's a moonshiner?" I asked.

"A person who distils and sells illegal whisky. Don't you have them in England. There were hundreds here at the time of the prohibition," Wendy replied.

Old Rob was watching us suspiciously. "It's a pity he had to catch the wild horse," Angus said. "Couldn't we come to some sort of bargain? You know, we'll keep our mouths shut if you will let us have the horse."

"Not possibly." Wendy replied. "My father buys whisky off him, so do several of our friends."

"There's nothing we can do then?" Angus asked, with a choke in his voice.

"Nothing. It's just our tough luck that he had to go and catch the horse, that's all." Wendy replied.

I looked at the Palomino and a great lump rose in my throat. He'll never be ours now, I thought.

Wendy rode forward. "Hiya, Rob," she said, holding out her hand. "I'm Wendy Miller."

They shook hands. Angus turned to me. "What happened to you?" he asked.

"I just got separated," I replied. I didn't want to

xplain how angry I had felt. It seemed childish now
nd silly.

"Well, it looks as though our dream's over," Angus said.
I wondered what Rob would do with the Palomino. He
nd Wendy were talking together like old friends.

"I should like to be a moonshiner. It must be jolly
xciting. I wish we had them in England," Angus
aid.

"There may be some in Scotland." I suggested. All the
eauty seemed to have gone from the day. The sun had
lisappeared; there were clouds in the sky. I gave Angus
Frances to hold, and talked to the Palomino, and his
enseness gradually vanished, and he sniffed my hands
nd seemed quite friendly.

"He's tamer already. Rob must be good with horses."
Angus said.

The clearing smelt of cut grass drying in the sun.
Somewhere a bird was singing a dreary little song about
the fall. I ran my hand down the Palomino's shoulder
which was hard, with plenty of muscle. His forearms
were long, his cannon bones and tendons short and strong.
He felt my hair with his lips and blew down my neck. I
saw that his hoofs were well-shaped, and that his pasterns
sloped.

"Be seeing you then," Wendy said. She mounted the
chestnut and said. "Let's go."

I took Frances from Angus and looked once more at the
Palomino. He was pawing the ground and watching us
with anxious eyes. I hated leaving him alone in the
clearing.

"Isn't there anything we can do?" I asked Wendy.

"Rob will sell him for a thousand dollars. That's his
price. I'm going to try Daddy. but I doubt that he'll go
as far as that. He thinks that horse is bound to be a
packet of trouble any way you look at him," Wendy
replied.

That's more than three hundred pounds, I thought, and
knew there wasn't a hope of Angus or I ever owning the

Palomino. We followed the little trail stumbling over the boulders and Angus said:

"At least we've found what we were looking for."

"What about something to eat?" Wendy suggested.

I realised then that Angus and I had forgotten to bring any lunch. But it didn't matter, because Wendy had brought enough for three. We sat on boulders and ate ham sandwiches and drank water from a spring—Rob's spring I guessed. We watered the horses and loosened their girths.

"This is great." Wendy exclaimed.

She didn't seem to mind about Rob having the wild horse, not like Angus and I did anyway. We could hardly speak for disappointment. I suppose having horses already made a difference. She didn't long for a horse of her own like we did.

"Who do you think will buy him from Rob?" Angus asked.

"Probably some old dealer or a circus, I guess." Wendy replied.

We finished lunch and rode on and behind us echoed plaintive neighs from the clearing.

"He's so terribly lonely," I said.

Our horses answered the Palomino. Soon the mountain echoed with the sound of neighs.

"Poor old Rob. He can't be liking the din," Wendy said.

"You mean everyone will start looking for the wild horse around his cabin?" Angus replied.

"And then they'll find out about his distilling," I added, and suddenly I began to feel excited because there seemed hope at last on our horizon.

"He'll probably take him down to-night and sell him," Wendy told us. "He's got plenty of connections and he always works at night."

"But surely every moment he keeps him is dangerous," I cried.

"He may think it's worth it for a thousand dollars," Wendy replied.

"How did he catch him?" Angust asked.

I imagined Rob and the Palomino coming down the mountains together.

"In some sort of snare connected to a tree. He's pretty smart," Wendy replied.

I thought of the Palomino struggling in a snare.

"He says he's quiet enough once he's caught," Wendy told us.

We came to the sandy road and now the neighs from the clearing were faint and distant. Our horses hardly bothered to reply. It really seemed that the Palomino was lost to us for ever. I wished now that I had never left the others—we would still have had some hope left then.

We came to the gas line, and I thought of the Palomino in a dealer's yard. "Do cheer up. There are other horses in the world," Wendy said.

But they're not the same, I thought. He has courage and speed; he's beautiful and alive; he's a horse in a million.

"Listen," cried Angus. "Stand still, can't you?"

I halted Frances. "What is it?" asked Wendy.

"Can't you hear? There's a horse coming," Angus cried,

I listened then and heard the gentle sound of distant hoofs pounding on a sandy road.

"He's coming. He's loose. Hurray, hurray," cried Angus, looking quite delirious with happiness.

Frances neighed. "It's too good to be true." I cried.

"I knew he wouldn't dare keep him," exclaimed Angus.

"He may have broken loose," Wendy said.

We stood and waited in an agony of excitement. The hoofs came steadily nearer. The chestnut neighed and then crashing along the trail came the Palomino. None of us could speak for a moment. He looked superbly beautiful; he still wore a head collar from which dangled

97

D

a piece of rope. He stopped with a snort about ten yards from where we stood.

"Let's ride on. Maybe he'll follow us," Wendy suggested.

"Yes, that's the best idea," agreed Angus.

We rode on along the trail and the wild horse followed.

"I don't suppose we'll ever know whether he broke the rope or Rob cut it," Angus said.

"Knowing Rob, I'm betting on the first," Wendy replied.

There was evening in the air and a faint mist which might become a fog before nightfall.

"He'll be much easier to catch with a head collar." Angus said cheerfully.

"You make him sound like quite an ordinary horse," I replied.

"Pity you had to pull the corral down. We could do with it now," Wendy said.

We came at last to the valley. "He's still following," Angus told us, looking back.

"This is the crucial moment," I said.

"You know we've lost the dogs?" Angus asked.

"Holy smoke, I'd forgotten all about them." Wendy replied. "Daddy will be furious."

"Will we have to go back?" I asked.

"We can't possibly look for them now," Angus cried.

"We'll darn well have to," Wendy replied.

"But what about the Palomino?" I asked.

Wendy turned the chestnut. "He'll have to wait. I can't leave the dogs in the mountains." she replied.

I felt a terrible, bitter wave of disappointment. It was so awful turning back, when we were nearly home with the Palomino just behind us. Wendy suggested that she should search for the dogs alone, but Angus and I wouldn't agree. The Palomino followed us for a time while we called, "Susie, Cop, Susie, Cop," until our throats were dry. But presently he grew tired of our wandering and cantered away into the dusk. The trails grew steadily arker. Our horses were tired and longed to turn for home. Angus wanted to give up the search. "They may have gone home for all you know," he kept telling Wendy. At last, she gave in and we turned our horses towards the valley, and they hurried, thinking of feeds of oats and warm stables.

The lights from houses shone like stars in the valley. The headlights from cars lit up the distant highway. We cantered down the rocky hillside, and jumped a wall.

Angus and I rode with Wendy to the Millers' house. because we wanted to know whether the dogs had returned on their own. Mrs. Miller was waiting for us between the pillars by the front door.

"My, what have you been doing?" she called.

Wendy explained about the moonshiner and the dogs. I waited anxiously. I knew we were terribly late. I dreaded the reception we might receive at home.

"They returned hours ago. Your parents have been calling us; you'd better get going, Jean," Mrs. Miller said.

So it was all unnecessary. I thought; instead of leaving the Millers' house at this moment. we might have been making the Palomino captive at home. Fate's against us, I decided dismally, saying good night to Mrs. Miller and Wendy.

Angus and I tore home.

"I can't see why we're always so silly," Angus said, as we neared the dirt road.

"Well, is wasn't our fault Wendy lost the dogs," I said.

Fortunately Mummy and Daddy weren't really angry. Mummy said we must try and be more considerate. Daddy told us to try and be our age and think of other people occasionally. We told them about losing Cop and Susie and they agreed that we couldn't have left Wendy to search alone. They were terribly interested in Rob, the moonshiner, and Daddy said he'd like to try some of his whisky.

Angus and I put the horses away as the moon ros
above the valley.

"I wonder where our phantom horse is now," Angu
said.

"It's wonderful to know that he can still be ours,"
replied, imagining myself cantering beneath the moon
jumping the walls and 'coops,' seeing a flaxen mane an
golden ears in front of me.

CHAPTER TEN

ANGUS AND I only rode the ponies quietly on Sunday
We cleaned their tack and ate peaches during the after-
noon. In the evening Wendy appeared and we practised
baseball on the lawn.

The next week passed very slowly. School was no
longer a novelty, and Angus seemed to be for ever fighting
with the other boys. A girl called Susan threw a boulder
at me when we had an argument, and I knocked her over
and sat on her. So gradually the other children ceased to
jeer at our English ancestry. Wendy taught me how to
wrestle and I found I could hold my own with any of the
girls of my age. The next week-end it rained. Angus and
I rode, but Mrs. Miller made Wendy stay indoors, much
to her annoyance. All this time we heard nothing of the
wild horse. In the mountains the leaves were falling from
the trees; the low land was wet and muddy; people began
to feed corn on the cob to the horses (commonly known
as corn in America).

Mr. Miller sent over a truckload of corn to Mountain
Farm; it was very like the corn on the cob one can buy
in England, only harder and more golden.

"Don't feed them more than two or three ears a day
to begin with. It's very heating," Mr. Miller told us.

When we tried stripping the corn off a cob, we found

looked very like English maize. The bay mare was going much better now, and we built jumps in the paddock out of the remains of the corral. Frances improved and soon she would canter on either leg, rein back quite decently and jump a three-feet course without any hesitation.

Angus and I tried to improve our riding. We wanted to be much better by the time we caught the wild horse. We thought it would be too awful if when, at last he was ours, we couldn't ride him. Mummy and Daddy thought our certainty of one day owning the wild horse was over-optimistic and silly. They frequently pointed out that since half Virginia had failed, there was little reason to suppose we would succeed. We didn't listen to such dismal suggestions, but continued to school each other diligently in the paddock for half an hour every evening.

Wendy didn't think much of our schooling efforts. She said that galloping about the mountains would teach us more, and that we were making the horses stale. We didn't listen to her either.

Then on an October evening when Angus and I had finished riding and were just starting our 'prep,' Wendy telephoned. I answered and she came to the point straight away.

"I say, Jean, we've just realised it's the opening meet of the Jameson hounds next Saturday, and we just wondered whether you and Angus would like to come along with us," she said.

The Jameson hunt is one of the smartest packs in Virginia. The subscription is something like three hundred pounds. I wondered what the cap would be.

"We'd love to. But I shall have to ask Mummy and Daddy. Is the meet near? I mean, can we hack?" I asked.

"Don't be dumb. Your horses can travel with mine in the truck." Wendy replied.

"Thanks awfully. Hold on a sec'," I said.

Mummy was reading. Daddy was writing letters. I was a bad moment to ask a favour. "It's Wendy," I said "She wants to know whether we can go to the opening meet with her on Saturday." Angus had listened to the telephone conversation.

"She will take our horses with hers in their truck," he added.

"What's the cap?" Daddy asked.

"Who'll look after you?" Mummy inquired.

"Why do we need looking after? We hunted on our own in England." Angus said.

I could hear Wendy talking into the receiver in the hall.

"I forgot to ask," I replied.

"You'd better find out then," Daddy told me.

I rushed back to the telephone. I suddenly wanted to hunt terribly badly. "Hallo," I shrieked. "Daddy wants to know who'll look after us, and what's the cap?"

"Heavens above, you're not kids of six!" Wendy said, and I thought there was scorn in her voice. "Daddy will be following in the station wagon; and you'll be our guests, so there won't be any caps."

"Thanks awfully. It's terribly nice of you." I replied.

"Oh, forget it," she said, and she sounded bored. I imagined her thinking, molly-coddled English children! Wendy can be very scornful.

I rushed back to my parents and cried, "There's no cap to pay. Mr. Miller will look after us."

Daddy said, "Do speak more slowly."

I repeated when I had said, adding that we were to be the Millers' guests for the day.

"I must say that's very good of Charlie," Daddy remarked.

Wendy was still talking to the receiver in the hall. I thought. in another moment she'll be fed up and ring off.

I said, "She's still holding on."

Daddy turned to Mummy and said, "What do you
102

think, Angela?" in that maddeningly slow way parents sometimes have when you're in a hurry.

"I don't see why they shouldn't go, if only they can be sensible," Mummy replied.

I rushed to the telephone. "Yes, we can go. Thank you so much," I cried.

"Hurray, that's great. See you to-morrow at school," Wendy said.

I felt quite limp when I had put down the receiver. I had never imagined that we should hunt—not in my wildest dreams, and certainly not with the Jameson hounds. I stood by the telephone seeing hounds drawing a tiny covert, myself riding Frances, Angus well mounted on the bay mare. Oh. we are lucky! I thought, to think that we're really going to hunt in America.

Angus was overjoyed. Only our parents were dubious. "Remember it's better to go round a fence rather than risk a broken neck," Daddy said.

"We will really try to be sensible," Angus replied, and he sounded as though he really meant it.

I remembered the last time he had promised the same thing. And this time he really will, I told myself.

For the rest of the evening Angus and I could think of nothing but hunting. The next morning we rose early and groomed the ponies for hours. We collected information about the Jameson hounds at school. We discovered that they belonged to a very rich family called the Smythes and had been started in 1908. We also discovered that the Smythes were the owners of the wild horse.

Wendy told us that we must bring our horses over to the Millers' place by ten o'clock. The meet was quite close, but no one seemed to consider hacking.

Angus and I spent a great deal of time sponging and pressing our riding clothes. We could think of nothing but the meet and we increased our horses' oats and corn by several double handfuls and ears. Our parents decided to attend the meet. They also invited people to stay for the week-end.

The weather stayed warm. Thursday arrived and w
found that Frances had a loose shoe. A terrible search fo
a blacksmith ensued. At last we heard of a coloured one
who came in an enormous car and shod Frances at sever
o'clock in the evening. His charge was ten dollars, which
is a little over three pounds. We were all horrified by such
expense.

Friday was warm with a few scattered showers. I was
kept in after school because I hadn't attended to a history
lesson. Angus was furious; and he and Wendy and Mr.
Miller had to wait for me. And though they were all
very nice about it, I felt horribly guilty.

Angus and I rode for about twenty minutes when at
last we reached home. Then we cleaned the tack, which
wasn't very dirty. We groomed the ponies until dark,
and gave them three ears of corn each and a large feed
of oats.

"I hope they won't be too fresh," Angus said. "I wish
we were hacking to the meet."

"What sandwiches would you like? Ham, egg or
cheese?" Mummy asked, when we entered the kitchen.

"Ham, please," we both answered.

It seemed funny to be preparing for hunting again.
Particularly so far from home. I couldn't believe that we
would ever really arrive at the meet. It all seemed a little
too good to be true.

Angus charged about the house collecting his clothes
and singing "John Peel." Mummy gave us lots of advice;
I decided that we must get up at six, have mucked out by
six-thirty and have the horses ready by nine. Angus said
I was mad and if we got up at seven we would still have
plenty of time. In the end we agreed to split the difference
and set the alarm clock for six-thirty.

I don't think I slept much that night. I was terribly
excited, and a little apprehensive because I knew that
neither the bay mare nor Frances had hunted before. I
was determined that Angus and I would behave sensibly;
I dreaded another accident, but would our mounts be

ensible? I wondered, tossing and turning in bed. I could see the bay mare in my imagination, kicking other members of the field, cantering sideways. barging into horses with her quarters. Frances. I decided, would probably buck. I saw myself falling off in front of the entire field. In more optimistic moments I saw both our horses behaving beautifully, and us patting them enthusiastically at the end of the best run for many seasons. I dreamed about school when I finally fell asleep. Angus and I were playing baseball and then suddenly the baseball bat became a hunting horn and we were running madly across fields in pursuit of hounds. I wakened to the shrill ring of the alarm clock.

The morning was warm and still. I shrieked at Angus, dressed quickly and rushed down to the stable. Frances was lying down. The bay mare was grazing over her door at the new day. I gave them both water and a little hay. Frances was very dirty and I had to fetch hot water and soap from the kitchen. Angus appeared still half asleep. "Thank goodness my mount's bay," he said.

I washed Frances. The sky turned blue; the sun shone. It was like a warm March day in England.

"I'm afraid it's going to be too bright for much scent," Angus said.

We had decided to plait the horses' manes. I had two reels of thread for Frances, one chestnut, one white. We mucked out the boxes and then we dashed indoors and gobbled a breakfast of scrambled eggs on toast. We groomed the horses for ages and then we plaited, which took hours. Frances had a thin wispy mane. The bay mare's was thick. I sewed some plaits three times and they still looked awful, and then it was too late to re-sew any of them. By this time the bay mare had six enormously fat plaits and a forelock; Frances had seven thin ones and lots of wispy hair which had refused to become plaits. We gave the horses feeds and hurried indoors. It was ten to nine.

"We mustn't be late at the Millers'," Angus said.

Mummy had kindly made us sandwiches, and Dadd was amusing the week-end guests, who had just got up. One of them seemed to be called Liz and the other wa Robbie. Liz was wearing elegant lounging pyjamas anc Robbie was still in his dressing-gown—or what American: call a robe. They were asking for tomato juice for break fast. Poor Mummy looked distraught. She never ha: liked having week-end guests. I was glad that I was hunt-ing. I wondered whether Liz and Robbie would appear a the meet in their lounging pyjamas and robe. I still fel terribly excited.

Angus and I bridled our mounts at half-past nine. Our pockets were stuffed with sandwiches. We mounted and rode across the valley and Frances felt fresh and very gay, and the bay mare jogged and wouldn't walk. We could see our parents and Robbie and Liz waving by the back door.

"Well at least we aren't late so far," Angust said cheerfully.

Wendy was waiting for us in the stable-yard. She was dressed in light-coloured breeches, a black coat, a hunting-tie and black boots. She wore a bowler and carried an extremely elegant hunting-whip. Suddenly, our clothes seemed all wrong and rather shabby. Wendy's hair was in a net; her clothes looked almost new. Somehow I hadn't expected Wendy to be smart. Normally she would ride in anything—worn jeans and sneakers, tattered breeches and decrepit Newmarket boots. A flying jacket, a leather waistcoat, a colossal jersey. moccasins and old slacks and a checked shirt. I was speechless for a moment. So was Angus.

"Hi, you're in fine time. The truck's out in front," Wendy said.

"You look frightfully smart. Really super," Angus exclaimed.

"I feel awful. I'm sure my coat doesn't fit. It was Mummy's," she replied.

106

"Does it matter that we're wearing crash caps? You see, we haven't got bowlers," I asked.

"Of course not. Everybody will think you're about ten anyway." Wendy answered with a grin.

"I don't think that's much of a compliment," Angus said.

Although Wendy had said 'truck' from the beginning, I was surprised to see Pete's chestnut standing in an open truck. I had imagined a horse-box. The truck looked small for three horses.

"What's the matter? Don't you like our transport?" Wendy asked.

I could see Angus looking at the four rails which served for sides. I saw that there was no ramp.

"How do we get them in?" I inquired.

"Just by leading. How the heck do you think? That's why the truck's against the hill. We have got a loading ramp, which we drive the cattle down; but we find the horses like jumping in off the hill a whole lot more," Wendy replied, leading the way towards the truck.

I was glad Mummy hadn't seen our form of transport.

Pete's chestnut was wearing a rug. His mane wasn't plaited, but I saw that he had been clipped. Joe was by the truck and he grinned and waved when he saw us.

"He's coming too," Wendy said.

Angus looked at the chestnut. "I feel very hobbledehoy, don't you, Jean," he whispered. "Wendy's so smart. Do you think everyone else will be?"

"I expect so; but it doesn't really matter," I answered without conviction.

"I can't think why we didn't have the horses clipped." Angus said.

"It would have been awfully difficult and we would have had to buy rugs," I replied.

"I wish we were rich. It didn't seem to matter in England, but it does here," Angus said.

"You mean us being rather poor?" I asked. "You can't say we're really poor when we've got a car."

"Everyone has a car over here. Most people have two," my brother replied.

"Do stop grumbling," I said. "We're jolly lucky to be going hunting at all."

Joe took Frances and, after a little persuasion, she jumped into the truck. He tied her to one of the rails by her reins, which made Angus raise his eyebrows. The bay mare was more difficult. She ran backwards and reared and oats had to be fetched and Mr. Miller appeared on the scene and everyone started to give each other instructions. Mrs. Miller appeared and took photographs, which didn't seem to help much. Then, quite suddenly, the bay mare decided to be sensible and jumped calmly into the truck, and stood still beside Frances. Mr. Miller cheered.

Joe tied her to the rails by her reins and then he climbed into the cab. Wendy. Angus and I climbed in with the horses, though Mrs. Miller seemed nervous and thought we would be better in the front with Joe.

We waved madly as Joe drove the truck down the hill. I must say it didn't feel at all safe. The floorboards seemed loose and the rails at the sides were only fastened by a few nails. I hoped we wouldn't meet Mummy and Daddy before we reached our destination. The horses were restless, and I untied Frances, because I didn't want her to break her reins before we reached the meet.

Soon we were travelling along the highway; air rushed at our faces and once Angus nearly lost his hat. Wendy started to tell us about the Master of the Jameson hounds.

"He's madly handsome and has a sweet wife. He hunts hounds himself and he's really great on a horse. He's strict though, so be careful," she warned us.

I imagined a tall, slim figure in pink sitting astride an enormous well-bred hunter. He'll look disdainfully at our hacking-jackets, I thought gloomily, and he'll send us home when he sees our crash caps.

"He's terribly nice though," Wendy added as an after-thought.

CHAPTER ELEVEN

THE MEET was outside a large, low, rambling white house. In front was a sweep of gravel; behind were the stables where we unloaded our horses on to a manure heap, there being no loading ramp or hill near-by. The stables were marvellous: built in a square, painted white with a veranda running round the entire yard, they were quite unlike anything I had seen before. Inside the boxes were partly tiled: and the saddle-rooms were magnificently arranged with marvellous sinks and elegantly tiled floors. Coloured grooms were rushing backwards and forwards with tack and stable rubbers and tins of hoof oil.

"Isn't it all super?" Angus exclaimed.

I was looking at other horses' plaits. I thought ours looked very amateurish in comparison.

"Let's go. I hope Daddy's here," Wendy said. She seemed nervous and ill at ease now that we had arrived. "I hope the horses behave," she added.

Joe held our stirrups while we mounted. Frances napped towards the bay mare. We rode round to the front of the house.

There wasn't a large field by English standards. An elegant parlourmaid in uniform was offering coffee to the twenty or thirty horsemen assembled, and to the spectators who had arrived in cars. There were plenty of grooms; but no interested locals like one sees at English meets. It was very much a class affair, and nearly all the horsemen were marvellously turned out in scarlet and toppers. There was one woman riding sideways, who had blue hair which she wore in a bun under a top hat. Another

woman wore a coat with swallow tails. There was only
one rider in ratcatcher besides ourselves and she was an
English girl of about eighteen.

Hounds looked marvellous and all very much of a size.
The Master rode a large chestnut. The one whipper-in
was mounted on a bay. Wendy nodded to one or two
people; then Mr. Miller appeared and said, "You'd better
meet the Master."

There was no sign of Mummy and Daddy.

We followed Mr. Miller across the drive and he introduced us as "Two visitors from England."

Mr. Smythe smiled and said, "I hope we give you a
good day."

Angus said, "Thank you, sir."

Then Frances started to run backwards into hounds and
we hastily retreated.

"It's not nearly as friendly as an English meet," Angus
complained.

"It's probably only because we're strangers," I said. But
I thought of meets at home in England. I remembered
the crowds outside a country pub, mothers with prams,
children on bicycles, old age pensioners, young men on
motor bikes, shabby foot followers. Everyone in the village would be there and everyone would know everyone
else. There would be a fleet of cars and bicycles and foot
followers behind the field when we set off to draw the
first covert. There would be cameras clicking and a great
feeling of comradeship. Here, in America, the sport
seemed to belong only to a selected few. There was something missing, I thought, watching the parlourmaid hand
Mr. Miller a cup of coffee.

"There's Mummy," Angus said.

Our parents had arrived with their week-end guests,
who had changed into suitable clothes. Daddy came across
to where we stood.

"Where's Mr. Miller? I thought he was going to look
after you," he said.

I suddenly had an awful empty feeling in the pit of my

tomach. It was obvious that Daddy expected Mr. Miller
o be mounted. It's funny how we just can't do anything
ight, I thought.

"He's over there," Angus replied, pointing to where
Mr. Miller stood talking to a fat man on a small, bay
horse.

"But he's not even dressed for riding. How can he look
after you without a horse?" Daddy asked.

*Frances banged the woman with the blue hair with
her quarters*

Mummy appeared. "Where's Charlie?" she inquired.

"He's following in the station wagon. He always does. I
replied.

"I don't see how he can look after you when he's in a
car," Daddy said.

"It doesn't sound a very good arrangement to me," Mummy said.

"I suppose we can't do anything about it now," Daddy told us, "but I wish you had explained the situation to us before."

"We didn't really think about it," I replied truthfully. "Wendy just said that he would look after us and would be following in the station wagon."

"They're just going to move off," Angus said, looking at hounds.

"Well, do try and be sensible," Mummy said.

"I'll keep an eye on them," Wendy promised.

"Remember they don't even know the country," Daddy said.

The Master blew a short toot on the horn. We rode away down the drive in bright sunlight. The sky was still blue. It was the beginning of our first hunt in America.

A crowd of second horsemen followed the field at a respectful distance. We crossed a road and passed through an open gate into a large meadow. Everyone started to canter then; the bay mare bucked; Frances banged the woman with the blue hair with her quarters. Wendy said, "Don't thrust, Jean." and I felt furious because I had hunted quite often in England and didn't wish to be told elementary things by Wendy.

The first covert was a small wood. Frances was sweating when we halted. and Angus was having trouble with the bay mare.

"Why the heck don't you keep away from everyone else?" Wendy asked.

I tried to move Frances, but she clung to her stable companion and the bay mare clung to the other horses. "It's all very well for you to talk. You're on an experienced hunter," I replied.

"There's no need to get mad. I'm only trying to help," Wendy said.

Frances banged the blue woman again and she cried, "Heavens sakes, keep that mare still."

The bay mare lashed out sideways at a tall man on a large grey. Angus said, "Sorry, sir."

I realised that I wasn't enjoying my hunt much so far. The English girl in ratcatcher grinned and called, "What are they—young horses?"

Then I heard someone say, "We're going to organise a real round-up on Monday," and my mind leapt to attention.

"I hear he's as wily as a grass snake," the man on the grey replied.

"We'll take him dead if not alive," someone said; and I suddenly felt quite empty, because I knew they were talking about the wild horse. I glanced at Angus and saw that he too was listening.

"He's done too much damage already. He's quite nuts. He's got three of Sam's horses with him right now," the tall man said.

There's only to-morrow. I thought desperately, and then a hound spoke.

"I suppose his darned pelt will be worth a few cents," someone said with a laugh.

"Well, let's hope it doesn't come to shooting. I don't like the idea of putting a bullet in any horse's skull." the tall man replied.

Another hound picked up the line. "They've found," the English girl said.

Frances started to fidget. I thought of Monday. I saw scores of riders approaching the mountains. Someone hollered. I heard the horn and suddenly I was galloping with everyone else, feeling a faint breeze in my face, hearing the 'gone away' echoing across the sunlit Virginian fields. We came to a wall which Frances took in her stride; we swung left and there was a hill and at the bottom a large line of rails. "They're too big for our horses," Angus cried, suddenly beside me.

"Perhaps someone will break them," I replied.

Wendy was in front. She seemed to have forgotten all about us. Frances had settled down.

I watched the Master jump the rails without changing the pace of his hunter. Other people followed.

"They certainly jump," Angus said.

Beyond the rails was more grassland and in the distance a wood. I didn't think the hounds spoke as much as an English pack; and the Master didn't blow his horn again. But the country was far more open, so I suppose it wasn't necessary.

A grey horse broke the rails right in the centre of the fence. Angus gave a cheer. Presently we were galloping towards the wood. Hounds checked and we saw a long line of cars coming towards us across the fields. Frances was blowing quite a bit and her long coat dripped with sweat. I dismounted and loosened her girths. Wendy came across.

"Are you okay?" she asked.

"Wizard," I replied.

"Have you heard about the round-up? They're going to try and catch the wild horse on Monday. Isn't it awful?" Angus said.

"Who are they?" Wendy asked.

The stream of cars had arrived. People were getting out and hailing friends.

"Everybody here as far as I can make out," Angus replied and there was despair in his voice.

"Are you kids all right?" Mr. Miller called, looking enormous in a camelhair coat and Newmarket boots.

"Yes, thank you," I replied. Then a hound spoke. I pulled up my girths and mounted. There was a sudden burst of music as the whole pack picked up the line. We heard the 'gone away' as we galloped towards the wood.

"They've broken on the far side." someone said. We jumped a smallish stile and then we were in the wood. I forgot everything but the feel of Frances's stride, the rushing air in my face. the music of hounds in full cry.

We slid down a bank and jumped a stream and then we were out of the wood and in open country again. Hounds were running very fast and making very little noise. A couple of big hunters swept past Frances; in front was a wall; beyond were more huge meadows. I patted Frances and wondered how long she would stand the pace. We jumped the wall and I noticed a ditch beneath as we landed. I saw that the bay mare was over as we galloped on across grassland; in the distance a large house stood beyond a terrace gazing towards the Blue Ridge Mountains. It looked completely deserted.

"That's the place Bill Matthews built for his first wife. He had to build another for his second wife, so now it stands empty," said Wendy, suddenly beside me. I was appalled by such extravagance. The next moment Wendy was past and galloping close to a big chestnut horse, ridden by a man in scarlet.

We turned left and galloped through a gateway and across a track. Hounds were well in front of the whole field. I don't think I'd ever seen a pack run so fast before. We jumped a 'coop' set in a wire fence. We passed a herd of Angus cattle. I was with the tail end of the field: Angus was just behind. The scene in front was like a modern sporting print thought not really English in appearance, because there weren't any hedges.

The field doubled back because of wire, which enabled us to gain a little ground. The sun was shining still and I was surprised that there was any scent at all.

We came to a stream wide and treacherous and for a moment Frances hesitated. then we were over and galloping across grass again.

As we jumped a low flight of rails, nearly ten minutes later, I realised that Angus and I were losing ground. Slowly the pack and the field mounted on fast, fit hunters were drawing away from us. Frances was tiring; the bay mare was dark with sweat.

"Let's slow down." I shouted to Angus. "It's their first

115

hunt after all. We don't want to spoil them for the rest of the season."

We pulled up our horses and it was awful watching the hunt disappearing into the distance. But it was some consolation to know that we were doing the right thing.

"What now?" Angus asked.

"Home, I suppose," I replied.

"I wish there were more and bigger woods," Angus said.

"It's marvellous country for a fast fit horse," I replied.

We couldn't hear the pack any more. It was dismal standing together in the vast Virginian countryside without a soul in sight. There wasn't even a cow within a mile of where we stood.

"I hope you know the way home, because I don't," Angus said.

"I don't, but maybe the horses do," I replied hopefully.

"Remember they travelled to the meet by truck," Angus said. So we were lost, I realised with dismay. All Virginia seemed to stretch before us. "Hell's bells," I cried. "Why can't we ever do the right thing?"

"It's not as though we don't try," Angus retorted. I saw us returning in gathering darkness: our parents waiting, anxious and angry, scanning the landscape, imagining ghastly accidents.

"If we find the truck, we only have to wait for Wendy," I said.

"Quite—if we find the truck," Angus replied.

"Well, we must know the way we came," I cried, turning Frances.

We jumped the low flight of rails again. We rode across endless grassland, and then somewhere we went wrong. We came to a ploughed field, and we both knew that we hadn't crossed plough before during the day.

"Hell's bells," I said again.

"Personally, I think it's entirely Wendy's fault. After

116

all, she was supposed to look after us," Angus exclaimed angrily.

The plough was dry and powdery. The sun had moved considerably since morning. "I guess it's about two o'clock," I said.

We ate our sandwiches. We jumped a wall and found ourselves riding across grass again.

"Americans don't think. That's the trouble," Angus said.

"You mean Wendy didn't think far enough to remember that we were on young horses?" I asked.

"Exactly," Angus replied.

"I suppose she'll guess that we're heading for the truck. There's not much else we could do," I said.

We rode through a gateway into another grass field. We saw a stream and a wood, but they weren't the ones we knew. We jumped some rails and found to our horror that we were back in the ploughed field. An awful feeling of helplessness assailed us then.

"We're just riding in circles," Angus cried desperately. I saw us still riding aimlessly at midnight. Oh, why did we ever go hunting? I thought miserably. We might have known everything would go wrong.

"What do we do now?" asked Angus, and there was anger as well as despair in his voice.

"Let's see what the horses think," I suggested. I dropped Frances's reins and prayed that she would know the way home, but she only ate the grass which grew at the edge of the plough. There was a feeling of late afternoon, which hung heavily in the air.

"We might as well give up and die," Angus said.

"Don't be so defeatist," I replied. "I wish we had a compass."

"Well, we haven't, so that's that," Angus replied.

"There's no need to be so cross." I said.

"I'm not. I'm just thinking of the row we're going to get into when we eventually return home." Angus answered.

"Well, this time it really isn't our fault," I replied, wondering how long Wendy would keep the truck waiting for us.

"This just wouldn't happen, hunting in England. A crowd of foot followers would have set us on the right road hours ago," Angus said.

"We'd better try again," I answered.

The horses were bored now as well as tired. I think they knew that we were lost. We rode on and on and afternoon turned to evening; and then at last we reached a road. Angus gave a feeble cheer and the horses pricked their ears.

"Which way do we turn?" Angus asked.

Neither of us had ever seen the road before, but Frances seemed to know it. She turned left in a very definite manner and Angus said, "Thank goodness someone seems to know the way."

The road was narrow. It wandered between wood fences and past a few farms standing at the end of long drives.

We started to think about the wild horse as we followed the strange road. I thought of hunting him across the vast, well-fenced and little-wooded Virginian countryside. Then I remembered the approaching round-up and all my hopes and dreams seemed to die. I remembered that the Virginians would shoot him if they couldn't catch him, and there just didn't seem any point in hoping any more.

The shadows lengthened across the unknown road and Frances stumbled with weariness.

"I'm going to dismount and walk," I told Angus. He dismounted too and we walked steadily along the road in to the gathering dusk.

"If only they weren't going to shoot him," said Angus at last.

And I saw the Palomino falling as the bullet hit him and heard the cries of his pursuers. Then I remembered the Virginians' renowned love of horses, the stud farms

scattered across Virginia, and I knew then that the
Palomino had a chance.

"I don't believe they'll shoot him, not when the
moment comes," I said. "They're too fond of horses.
It would be different if he was old, or diseased or in
pain."

The shadows lengthened across the unknown road

"I hope you're right," Angus said.

We started to worry about Wendy then. Would she be
waiting for us? we wondered, or would she have returned
home and told everyone we were lost? Or was she still
hunting across the dusky fields? We both hoped that she
was still hunting or hacking home like us.

We came at last to a road which met our road at right
angles, and once again Frances knew the way. It was very
nearly dark by now. I thought of the tea waiting for us
in Mountain Farm, of warm welcoming lights and a hot

bath. Frances started to hurry. Perhaps we're gettin
near, I thought, peering into the dusk.

But I could see nothing familiar about the road; an
the trees on each side were strange to us, and so was th
faint outline of the valley below. The bay mare wa
tired. I could see it by the droop of her head and in th
way she walked. The road obviously meant nothing t
her. Angus and I were tired too, too tired to talk. W
ought to find a telephone, I thought. I imagined ringin
up Mountain Farm and Daddy answering. I wondered
why we hadn't thought of it before. I started lookin
for a house; but for ages we only passed wooden shack
with derelict gardens. Inside I could see large black fami
lies eating round a table, and though many coloured
people are rich, I could see that these were not, and I
knew they wouldn't have a telephone.

Frances still hurried. She seemed suddenly tireless. A
car passed with blazing headlights and our horses cringed
and blinked. There were lights ahead which showed us a
house silhouetted against the dark sky. We came to a
drive and, with a sudden rush, Frances swung down it as
though it was home.

"Where are you going?" yelled Angus. while I felt
quite sick with disappointment. So this was where Frances
had been leading us, I thought, not to Mountain Farm,
nor the Millers' place, but to a strange house, standing
near an unknown road. I suddenly felt twice as weary.
I couldn't see how we were ever to reach home, our
parents could wait all night for us and still we wouldn't
arrive. It must be one of Frances's previous homes, I
thought, staring furiously at the house ahead, and all the
time Angus kept calling. "Where are you going, Jean?
What *are* you doing?"

"There may be a telephone," I yelled back into the
darkness.

Frances hurried along the drive and turned left towards
the dim outline of a building. which I guessed was the
stable. A horse whinnied, and the bay mare raised her

head and answered. The stable was in darkness. We could just see three heads gazing at us over doors, as we turned towards the house. There were lights in the kitchen and a coloured woman opened the back door when we knocked. I explained our plight and she disappeared in search of someone.

"What are you going to do if they haven't got a telephone?" Angus asked.

"Find out where we are," I replied.

The coloured woman returned with a lean, little man in riding clothes and a checked waistcoat.

He said, "Hi," and then, "Gee, if it isn't Frances."

"We're trying to get home. She brought us here," I explained.

"I traded her with Charlie Miller over the other side—must be three years ago now," he said. "I traded her for the heck of a horse."

"Please have you got a telephone?" I asked.

"He jumped real good that horse. I sold him to a dealer in New York. I can't remember his name right now. Sure, I've got a telephone," he added, as though he'd only just thought of it. "Do you want to come inside."

The walls were hung with photographs of horses. There was a collection of hunting whips and polo sticks in the hall. The house smelt of cooking, leather and saddle soap.

The telephone was in a small front room where there were whisky bottles and beer bottles and a dozen or more glasses and tumblers. There were magazines, and a couple of books on riding lying on the table in the centre of the room.

Fortunately, I knew the number of Mountain Farm. While I waited for the exchange to answer the owner of the house talked. He wanted to know where we came from, which pack we'd been hunting with, how we'd come by Frances. He told me that we were roughly fifteen miles from Mountain Farm, that we'd better leave

the horses with him and be fetched by car, and that hi
name was Jim Blackburn, and that his parents were Irish
Then the exchange answered and he left the room.

I saw that one of the magazines was called *The Chonicle*
and that there was an oil painting of a horse over the
mantelpiece, before Mummy answered.

I said, "It's Jean here. I'm terribly sorry we got lost.
We're fifteen miles from home and the horses are terribly
tired. We don't know where Wendy is."

"Thank goodness you've rung up. Wendy's just got
back. We were just about to send out a search party.
Where exactly are you?" Mummy asked, sounding
relieved.

"At Jim Blackburn's place," I replied. "He said he'll
put up the horses for the night."

"That's very handsome of him. But it still doesn't tell
me where you are," Mummy answered.

"Hang on. I'll find out," I said. I found Jim Blackburn
talking to Angus. They'd removed the horses' saddles.
The coloured woman was making coffee in the kitchen.
I persuaded Jim Blackburn to return to the telephone
and talk to Mummy, only by that time it had become
Daddy.

"Are they furious?" Angus asked, when Jim Blackburn
had finished directing Daddy and we were leading
the horses to two loose-boxes which were conveniently
empty.

"No, I don't think so," I replied. "I think that Mummy
was just pleased to know that we were still in the land
of the living."

We bedded down the boxes and fed and watered Frances
and the bay mare. Then Jim Blackburn took us indoors
and gave us each a mug of coffee with a dash of whisky,
and the coloured woman, who was fat and kind and called
May, put a plate of scrambled eggs in front of us, and a
loaf of fresh bread.

"Make yourselves at home. I'm slipping back out to

he barn to see that your hunters are comfortable," Jim Blackburn said.

Angus leapt to his feet and cried, "Can't we help?" But we were firmly told to stay where we were and eat what we were given. The eggs had been scrambled in a frying pan and were delicious. May found us butter and preserves and we ate vast quantities of bread. I didn't enjoy my coffee much; I don't like it anyway, and the whisky made it taste even worse than usual.

"I hope Mummy's rung up Wendy," Angus said. "It must have been terrible for her waiting by the truck."

The kitchen was lit by a single gas jet suspended from the ceiling. I felt incapable and sleepy. May seemed far away by the old-fashioned stove: the mugs hanging on the dresser were just a blur. Soon I slept sprawled across the table.

I wakened to the sound of voices and a hand on my shoulder. "Jean, wake up. Come on, it's time to go home," Mummy was saying. I had a crick in my neck and my legs felt stiff and heavy. For a moment I couldn't think where I was. Then it all came back.

"You've had a real good sleep," May said, with a smile which showed perfect teeth.

"It was that drop of whisky," Jim Blackburn said.

Mummy seemed to be thanking everyone. I stood up and looked around the kitchen.

"You've been asleep for ages," Angus said. "We've just been looking at the horses; they seem quite happy."

I was still too sleepy to talk much. I remember shaking hands and saying thank you to May and Jim Blackburn in a kind of daze. I stumbled into the car and fell instantly asleep. In my dreams I heard the steady drone of Angus's voice explaining things to Mummy.

Tea was still laid in the kitchen at Mountain Farm. But I was too tired to eat. I remember seeing that the clock on the window-ledge said nine o'clock and I asked Mummy if someone had told Wendy what had happened.

"Hours ago," she replied. "Daddy's over there now."

123

I remember falling into bed, feeling the pillow against my face and with it a wonderful sense of security. I remember Angus saying, "Well, I'm going to have a bath anyway," and Mummy's "Ssh." Then once again I slept and this time it was the dreamless sleep of complete exhaustion.

CHAPTER TWELVE

ON SUNDAY Joe drove Wendy and Angus and me over to Jim Blackburn's place in the truck. It was rather awkward meeting Wendy. Mr. Miller had been extremely angry when she returned without us and as a punishment she wasn't to ride for a week. We had learned this from Daddy. As a result Angus and I felt horribly guilty. In a way we knew that we were responsible for the punishment. Fortunately, Wendy isn't a person to harbour a grievance. She grinned when we met and called, "Sorry I let you down yesterday. I feel awful about it." After that we all blamed ourselves and set off in the truck in high spirits.

Wendy told us that she too had finished up miles from home on a tired horse. She had hacked back to the truck hoping to find us impatiently waiting; instead she had been met by a furious Joe, who said it was past six and he had his cow to milk when he got back. Wendy had insisted on waiting for half an hour, hoping that we might still turn up. She hadn't thought of ringing up home. Her father had telephoned Mountain Farm on her return. Later they had asked Mr. Smythe to ring up if we appeared at his place. Wendy hadn't been able to eat until after I had telephoned Mummy and everyone knew that we were at Jim Blackburn's place on the other side of the valley.

"I really think you had the worst time of all," Angus

said, when Wendy came to the end of her story. "At least our adventures were exciting."

"Our families have got together and none of us are to hunt again until the boys are back. As if they ever look after anyone," Wendy told us.

"We must get our horses clipped," Angus replied. "That is, if we can still have them next holidays."

"That's just the heck of it. I don't know just what to say. You see, I'm too big to ride my little roan any more and Daddy keeps saying we must have one of yours back," Wendy answered. She sounded apologetic and embarrassed. I said nothing. I hated the idea of losing either the bay mare or Frances, but we obviously couldn't keep both when Wendy had nothing to ride.

"Oh well, perhaps we'll have caught the Palomino by then. Anyway, don't worry, it won't be the first time we've managed with one mount between us; will it, Jean?" Angus asked.

"Far from it," I agreed.

"I wish we could think of some way of stopping the beastly round-up," Angus said. "If only we could get off school."

"I don't see what we could do then," Wendy replied.

"Jeopardise the whole expedition somehow," Angus answered.

"Hi, some of them happen to be friends of mine," Wendy said.

"I didn't say I was going to hurt anybody," Angus replied. I still felt sleepy. I think Wendy did too; there were dark rings under her eyes anyway and she kept passing her hand across her face, as though to ward off sleep.

It was another warm day. Jim Blackburn's place looked a haven of peace. A collie lay sunning himself in the stable-yard; the horses were blinking and dreaming over their box doors. We found Jim Blackburn cleaning a bridle in a little room leading off the kitchen. He greeted us gaily and we all walked to the stables together. Frances

and the bay mare looked tired. Their heads drooped an
they were each resting one hind leg.

"They're sound all right. I led them both out first thin
this morning. The bay mare's a wee bit stiff though,
Jim Blackburn told us.

We led the horses into the truck from a permanen
loading ramp. Then I made the little speech Mummy ha
suggested to me about paying for their board and lodging
But Jim Blackburn only laughed.

"Forget it," he said. "If I can't put up a couple o
horses for a night without asking a fee, I'd better quit."

So Angus and I thanked him all over again and he
showed us his horses, and the ones he was schooling for
other people, and a case filled with rosettes, and photographs of himself in his younger days. When at last we
were ready to go we were met by a furious Joe, who told
us that Sunday was his day off in the week and that it
was now twelve o'clock. Angus and I apologised, and
Wendy said, "Come off it, Joe. What about those odd
naps you take during the week?"

But Joe was in no mood to be teased. He climbed into
the cab of the truck and started the engine. We clambered
into the back half, just as it started with a jerk which
sent us stumbling among the horses' legs.

We all began to laugh when we were standing straight
again.

"One day Joe will murder someone," Wendy said.

We discussed the wild horse as we travelled home.
There seemed nothing we could do to stop the round-up.

"We'll just have to sit through school in agony, I
suppose," Angus said, "imagining the Palomino pitting
his wits against a bunch of hard-hunting Virginian men."

"I'm jolly well going to suggest we have to-morrow
off," I replied. "It's worth trying, anyway."

"We won't get it. Why should we?" Angus asked.

We unloaded the horses on a bank near Mountain Farm.
Wendy left with the truck. The week-end guests were still
at home. The kitchen smelt of Sunday lunch. Mummy

was making onion sauce. Liz was laying the table. Daddy and Robbie were knocking golf balls about on the lawn. It seemed a good moment to ask for a holiday from school, but I didn't know how to begin.

Finally, it was not until bed-time that I had the courage to ask that we might stay away from school the next day. The week-end guests had gone by then and a sudden peace had descended on Mountain Farm. We were sitting round a small fire in the dining-room and I asked with a sudden rush of words, and Mummy said, "Why on earth should you?" and Daddy said, "I do wish you would speak more slowly, Jean."

Angust explained about the round-up. "It's really tremendously important to us that we should forestall them," he finished.

"What do you mean by forestall?" Daddy asked.

"Find the wild horse before anyone else and drive him away from them," Angus answered promptly. I hadn't thought as far as that. I suppose it had been in Angus's head for some time.

"What a disgraceful idea. You really can't be so anti-social," Daddy said.

"Don't you want us to catch the wild horse then?" I asked.

"I don't much mind either way. But I'm definite about one thing—you are going to school to-morrow." Daddy replied.

I shall never forget Monday. On our way to school we met horsemen approaching the mountains by truck and horse-box, trailer and car. We also saw a few lone riders crossing the valley; and dogs and a couple of hounds. There seemed little chance for the wild horse against so many. There was one consolation; no one as far as we could see carried a gun or revolver. There was a breeze blowing and the air felt light and free.

"What a wonderful morning for a round-up. I wish I was ten years younger," Mr. Miller said.

"You're not so old. Let's have the radio on," Wendy suggested.

Mr. Miller drove very fast, relying on his brakes to save us should anything suddenly cross the road or dash out of a side turning.

My heart felt as heavy as lead. I was sure with the most complete certainty, that the Palomino would be captive before nightfall. I wondered whether the Millers would ask for the bay mare or Frances for the holidays. The remaining one would be very lonely living alone at Mountain Farm, I decided.

"Have you heard we're having a Hunt Breakfast on Christmas Day? The Jamesons are hunting. They've sent us an invitation," Wendy said.

"They always have an invitation meet on Christmas Day, and we thought it would be fun to give a Hunt Breakfast for everyone afterwards," Mr. Miller explained.

"It will be a kind of farewell too. Because we're spending a week in New York after Christmas," Wendy said. I felt Angus looking at me. It was the first time we had heard of anyone hunting on Christmas Day, or of the Millers visiting New York.

"Are they going to meet very early? I mean, how does breakfast fit in?" Angus asked.

I felt disappointed. I had been looking forward to hunting with Pete and Phil. Now it seemed that they would be leaving for New York almost as soon as they arrived.

"After the hunt of course. They meet about ten," Wendy replied.

It sounded more like a hunt lunch or tea to me. I wondered whether everyone ate breakfast dishes like haddock and kedgeree, or whether the drank fruit juices. I giggled and imagined the hunt staff eating cereals.

"Everyone comes still in their hunting kit. It's very colourful," Mr. Miller said.

I imagined muddy hunting boots trampling across the

Millers' polished floors, the clink of spurs. the pink coats.

"They send their horses home first of course," Mr. Miller said.

I thought of tired horses jogging home, climbing into vans and trucks: of negro grooms and second horsemen.

"They don't stay out long. Everyone's too darned keen to get back to their Christmas dinners," Mr. Miller told us.

"It's just a kind of tradition. We have our traditions too, you see," Wendy said.

"It won't be a big affair. The last time we had a Hunt Breakfast there were ninety-five guests. Do you remember, Wendy?" Mr. Miller asked.

"Sure," she replied.

"What are you going to New York for? Or is that being too curious?" Angus asked.

"To visit the theatres and the movies and the galleries. We go every year," Wendy replied. And now we had reached our school.

"Be good," Mr. Miller said, as we stepped out of the car and saw that we were late, and that the other children were all inside.

I had a great deal to think about during lessons: first and foremost there was the round-up, second came the Hunt Breakfast, lastly the Millers' visit to New York. I couldn't forget the round-up. When I was asked the answer to a simple piece of mental arithmetic I answered, "Palomino," and the class shook with laughter. It was with me during the entire morning; it lived with me throughout baseball in the afternoon. When I forgot it I saw the Hunt Breakfast and tables laden with food, and hounds drawing a covert on Christmas morning. After baseball, my mind wandered to New York. I tried to imagine the Millers in Times Square; Mr. and Mrs. in town clothes, Pete, Phil and Wendy reading the news in neon lights. I didn't envy them. I couldn't imagine anything worse than New York in January. I saw them wandering round immense picture galleries. I was certain that Pete would hate the visit. I couldn't imagine him understanding modern art, or enjoying meals in exotic cafés, or the lights of Broadway, or the noise, and the traffic and the crowds.

After school I was given a lecture by the headmaster. I had been reported three times for lack of attention. I tried to explain about the round-up and how important it was to me, but I don't think he understood. I didn't really listen to his lecture. I was longing to hear whether the wild horse was free or captive; nothing else seemed to matter. I heard that I was to stay in during break for the next five days, and I was only pleased that I wasn't to stay after school. I rushed out to the car where the others were waiting. Mrs. Miller had come to fetch us.

"What news?" I cried. "Have they caught him?"

"They hadn't by lunch time. I haven't heard anything since," Mrs. Miller replied.

"Isn't it awful? We still don't know," cried Angus in tones of exasperation.

"What did Sunny Jim say?" Wendy asked.

"Nothing much. Just that I'm to stay in during break for the next five days," I replied.

"Gee, tough luck," Wendy said. There were no horse vans or trucks on the road. They must be still driving him, I thought; they must all be terribly tired.

"How can we find out? We must find out," Angus asked.

"Find out what?" Mrs. Miller asked. "Oh, about that crazy horse. You're real obsessed about him, aren't you? It's not healthy, you know." she said.

We were nearly home now. I hoped that Mummy would have news. Someone must know whether they had caught the wild horse or not. There was a feeling of rain in the air. The sky was grey. There was no one riding across the valley. There wasn't a dog in sight. The Hereford cattle grazed undisturbed.

Angus and I found Mummy unpacking groceries.

"Is he caught?" cried Angus.

"Have you heard anything?" I asked.

Mummy knew what we were talking about. "I haven't heard a sound since early morning. I inquired at the post office just now and they said they hadn't seen any horsemen since lunch time," she replied.

We put our 'prep' on the table. "Tea's nearly ready," Mummy said.

Then the telephone bell rang. Angus answered. It was Wendy. I could hear her voice quite clearly from across the hall.

"We've just heard they haven't caught him. They're starting to go home now," she said.

I felt quite weak with relief. I leaned against the banisters, and heard Wendy say, "They nearly caught him at eleven o'clock this morning down by Hodge's Farm, but after that they never had a chance. They got the mares all right though."

I didn't listen any more. I suddenly wanted a cup of tea.

"Well, are you happy now?" asked Mummy, who had heard the conversation from the kitchen. "You really mustn't let it become an obsession with you," she continued. "After all, he's not your horse."

I wondered then whether Angus and I were really letting the wild horse become an obsession. It seemed odd that Mummy and Mrs. Miller should both say the same thing. Perhaps we are going nuts, I thought, and remembering how foolish I had been at school, I resolved to think less about the wild horse in future.

"Isn't it really supersonic?" cried Angus, bursting into the kitchen. "He's defeated them all. He's still free."

"I know. We heard," I said. He does sound rather obsessed, I thought, looking at my brother.

There were shop cakes for tea. Afterwards we rode and I told Angus about us being obsessed, and we decided to look it up in the dictionary; and we resolved to talk less about the wild horse.

"You see we're just becoming bores," I said.

"Quite. Like people who talk Army or Polo or even Hunting all the time." Angus replied.

"Or like the mothers who never stop talking about their children," I added.

It was warm and damp and quiet riding in the valley. We talked about the Hunt Breakfast as we rode and wondered whether we were to be invited.

Angus said that there would be things like calf's head, chicken's liver, minced heart and hot rolls to eat. I said there would be fish, eggs, ham and bread and butter, followed by waffles. I was being misled by the word breakfast. I think Angus was just trying to put me off. We agreed that there would be coffee to drink, and whisky.

The next three weeks passed slowly. Nothing happened. The wild horse seemed to have disappeared from the face of the earth. I received a long letter from Pete, full of questions about the cattle, which I couldn't answer. The days grew shorter. The Millers started to feed hay and corn to the cattle. Mummy began to mention Christmas.

On a cold dry Saturday we drove into Washington and bought Christmas cards and presents for friends and relations in England. Everything seemed rather expensive though not in comparison with American wages as Mummy pointed out. Most of the books in decent covers were between fifteen and twenty shillings, even quite ordinary novels. In the end we bought mostly handkerchiefs, and little bold horses on white stands saying 'Washington.' The Christmas cards were wonderful, but several of the most attractive were to *A Swell Sister,* or *To My Big Brother*, or with rhymes we didn't like.

Though we spent all morning shopping, lunched quickly off hot dogs in a soda fountain and shopped till tea time. we still hadn't bought enough presents when we started for home.

We spent the next two evenings doing up parcels for England and writing in Christmas cards. At last everything for England was posted and we started to think of each other's presents and what we could give the Millers.

December came and with it the first frost. There was still no sign of the wild horse in the mountains. Angus and I clipped the bay mare and Frances with the help of Joe and Wendy. Mr. Miller lent us horse rugs. Mummy and I made a Christmas pudding.

People didn't talk about the wild horse any more. It was as though he had suddenly ceased to exist.

We received an invitation to the Hunt Breakfast, which we all accepted. The Millers were busy ordering food and polishing the house. Normally they hired extra coloured staff and waiters for parties, but this time they couldn't because of it being Christmas.

Wendy bought some new clothes in Washington to wear in New York. Angus and I finished our Christmas shopping. I bought Angus an infuriating puzzle game where one had to engineer a little ball into a minute hole, and I bought him rather a small picture of three horses to hang over his bed. I chose a gay checked scarf for Mummy, and a large plain ashtray for Daddy. Finally I bought Wendy a wooden horse, Pete the latest map of the locality and Phil an ashtray like Daddy's. Mummy gave us a flower vase to give jointly to Mr. and Mrs. Miller. Then I remembered the coloured girl, who had just started to come in occasionally to help Mummy, and hastily bought her an artificial flower to wear in her hat.

At last term ended. We drove home singing madly. There were only five days now to Christmas. Late that evening Pete and Phil returned from school. They came down to see us at Mountain Farm. Phil seemed to have grown another foot. He towered above us all. Pete seemed older and more serious. Daddy gave them each a glass of beer and I found them some cake.

"So, you haven't caught the wild horse," Pete said.

"I hear he's been bumped off," Phil told us.

"That's the first we've heard of it," Angus replied.

"He can't have been," I cried, and I must have sounded

133

desperate, because suddenly everyone seemed to be look ing at me.

"Don't take him seriously, Jean. He doesn't know a doggone thing," Pete told me.

"It's only what I heard at the drug store when I stopped by for a Coke," Phil said.

It was nice to have Phil and Pete back again. I had forgotten how nice they could be. They sat sprawled in the kitchen talking while the dark December evening turned into night. At last they left, and Mummy said, "It's funny how boys of that age, wherever they come from, never seem to know when it's time to go."

"It's the same the whole world over," Daddy sang. I looked at the clock and saw that it was ten o'clock.

"We should have given them an egg or something," I said.

"I wish it was Christmas Eve," Angus exclaimed.

"It nearly is," Daddy said.

"Do you know we've been in America almost five months?" Mummy asked.

It doesn't seem so long as that, I thought, looking back across the months, remembering our arrival, our first view of Mountain Farm and the Millers, our first rides. But I felt immeasurably older. I didn't feel the same Jean who had left England nearly five months ago.

"I don't think I like the idea of hunting on Christmas Day," Daddy said.

I wasn't sure how I felt about it. But we hadn't received an invitation from the Smythes, so it didn't matter.

At last we went to bed; and, trying to sleep, I remembered the first time I had seen the wild horse, and my first glimpse of a Virginian moon; and the valley in the summer, warm and sunlit, and filled with the chorus of frogs in the lowlands.

CHAPTER THIRTEEN

SNOW FELL before Christmas. It came with a wind, and large drifts lay across the valley, and snowploughs were seen on the roads. The sky was a cold grey and there wasn't any sun.

Angus sang, "I'm Dreaming of a White Christmas," and I was glad that we hadn't been invited to the Christmas Meet, and sorry for the Millers. I hoped the weather wouldn't spoil their Hunt Breakfast.

The snow was dry, so we could still ride, though it wasn't really safe to jump. We hardly saw the Millers. We rode to their place two days before Christmas and found them packing presents in elaborate wrappings, tied with many-coloured bindings, decorated with artificial snow. They screamed when they saw us and cried, "Beat it. Don't look. We want privacy"; only they said '*pry*vacy' instead of privacy. Angus and I 'beat it,' and Pete cried after us, "Don't be hurt. We just happen to be wrapping your presents right now."

We didn't see the Millers again till Christmas Day. Two days before Christmas the weather changed; the sun shone and the sky was suddenly blue. In the valley the snow melted.

"They'll be able to hunt after all," Angus said with envy in his voice.

Wendy asked to have Frances back and we delivered her to Joe on Christmas Eve. There was nothing but dirty slush to show that there had been snow. The sun was scorching and we rode without coats. We took it in turns to ride the bay mare home across the valley. Every few minutes she neighed and Frances answered. "It's not going to be much fun having just one horse. We'll never catch the Palomino now," Angus said.

I looked across the dirty valley to the mountains faintly blue beneath the blue sky.

"I wonder where he is. No one ever seems to see him now," I answered.

It seemed strange to talk about the wild horse again afraid of being obsessed, we had hardly mentioned him for nearly six weeks.

"Perhaps Phil was right—perhaps he's been bumped off," Angus replied.

"Maybe he's moved to another valley," I said.

"Somehow I've stopped thinking he'll ever be ours. Everything seems so difficult," Angus said.

We put the bay mare in her box and she continued to neigh at one minute intervals.

"I wish she'd stop. Daddy will soon be fed up with the row," Angus exclaimed.

"No one should mind anything on Christmas Eve," I replied.

"I hate to think of her all alone. I wish we'd left her with Frances. I wouldn't want to spend Christmas in solitary confinement," Angus said.

"Maybe she'll cheer up soon," I replied. I felt foolishly dismal. I suppose it was because we wouldn't be hunting when the Millers were and because we had lost Frances.

We gave the bay mare a large feed before we went to bed hoping that it would make her sleep. Mummy wanted to give her aspirins, but we didn't because Angus said she wouldn't eat them. There was a bright moon shining through my window when I hung up my stocking. The weather was much too warm for Christmas. It was more like a summer night.

The bay mare had finished her feed and had started neighing again. Far away a cow was bellowing. I remembered Christmas at home; the feeling in the cottage on Christmas Eve; the excitement on Christmas morning, the unwrapping of presents, dinner in the tiny dining-room. Somehow Christmas in Virginia seemed quite different.

I wakened early, but not before the sun was shining in my room. My stocking was full and I seized it from the bottom of my bed before rushing into Angus's room. It was traditional that we should open our stockings together. There were all the usual things, even the tangerines in the toes of our stockings. The bay mare was still neighing. We sat on Angus's bed and ate chocolate, nuts and our tangerines. The sun was warm on our faces.

"It's going to be much too bright for hunting," Angus said.

"I agree with Daddy. I don't think Christmas Day and hunting go together."

"You know that's only wishful thinking. If we'd been invited you would think quite differently," Angus replied with a grin.

I wandered back to my room and dressed. Mummy and Daddy had decorated the house after we were in bed. The rooms were gay with coloured streamers, tinsel and glittering bells. A large Father Christmas beckoned me downstairs. I called softly to Angus to come quickly, and we stood and admired the decorations together before taking the bay mare a special Christmas breakfast. Later we took cups of tea to our parents in bed and wished them a happy Christmas.

We ate a breakfast of eggs and ham all together in the kitchen and then the moment had come to open our presents. They were waiting for us arranged on chairs in the dining-room. I opened Mummy's first and found a tough, sky-blue jersey. Daddy had given me a book on the different breeds of American horses, Angus had bought a wooden horse to stand on my bedroom chimney-piece. My aunts had sent a scarf and a pair of dashing yellow riding gloves. Daddy was delighted with his ash-tray, Mummy tried on her scarf, Angus dropped his picture but fortunately it did not break. We started to clear up the paper and string. "The Millers are giving you presents to-night," Mummy said. "I hope they aren't too elaborate."

We were to have dinner with the Millers, so we only ate a light lunch with a small helping each of the pudding Mummy and I had made.

The weather was changing rapidly. Gone was the blue sky and the bright sunshine. It was much colder; an unpleasant wind was blowing from the north-west.

"I hope they've had a nice morning's hunting," Mummy said.

"The scent should be better now there's no sun," Angus replied.

"I'm glad they aren't hunting around here. It would be awful to hear them and not to be hunting," I said.

"Awful," Angus agreed.

We washed up lunch and then we looked at our presents again and I put on my new jersey and scarf. Then we tried to cheer up the bay mare without succeeding.

"I should think they are home by now," Angus said, leaning against the stable door. "Wendy didn't think they'd stay out long."

"I bet Joe's furious," I said, remembering how cross he had been when he had driven us to Jim Blackburn's on a Sunday.

"I suppose they pay him overtime," Angus answered.

"They've probably given him a pig for Christmas," I said.

Presently Mummy called us in to dress. I put on my only respectable dress, a red corduroy. Angus changed into his suit, which he hates, because he thinks the seat looks shiny.

"I wish you had another dress, Jean. You'll clash with the hunting-coats," Angus complained.

I wished I was wearing breeches and boots and a black hunting-coat. I would have liked to have entered the Millers' house covered with mud and carrying a crash cap and hunting-whip.

"Do shut up," I said crossly. "You're not so suitable 'ourself."

"Well, you know I hate this suit," Angus replied. I hought, we're quarrelling on Christmas Day, how awful!

Daddy called, "Hurry up. We're late now."

The sky was quite grey when we stepped into the car.

"It's going to snow," Mummy said, burying her face in her overcoat.

Daddy turned on the heater. I suddenly didn't want to go to the Hunt Breakfast. I was sure we would look silly in our frocks and suits, and I was sure that everyone else would be talking about the run they had enjoyed in the morning, and Angus and I would have nothing to say at all. I never had liked parties much, unlike Angus who always wins all the prizes if there are any to be won. But there won't be prizes to-day, I decided dismally. It isn't that sort of party. It will be very grown-up with drinks on silver salvers and tough hunting men, and beautifully got-up American women.

It was snowing when we turned down the Millers' long drive. The lakes looked grey and cold. There was a cardinal perched on one of the walnut trees. We could see a collection of cars parked in front of the house.

"We're none too early," Daddy said.

Joe opened the car doors for us. When we were all standing in the porch beneath the pillars, he drove the car away.

Wendy opened the door for us. "Hi, you've come at last." she said.

She wasn't in hunting-clothes. She was wearing a dark green pinafore frock with an almost transparent blouse underneath. She had lipstick on and patent leather shoes.

"We were afraid we were late," Daddy apologised.

"But you're not. Lots of people haven't arrived yet," Wendy said. She left Daddy and Angus to take off their coats in the hall, Mummy and I followed her upstairs.

"We had a nice morning, but didn't do much. We neve[r] do on Christmas Day," Wendy told us.

I took off my coat and Wendy said, "What a prett[y] dress, I love the colour." I felt that she was trying ver[y] hard to be the perfect hostess.

"It's the only one I've got," I replied.

The house was full of people, some still in hunting-kit Pete and Phil called "Hallo," as we came downstairs They hadn't changed. They looked very dashing in thei[r] hunting-clothes.

Phil had a splash of mud across one cheek. Pete said, "Tomato juice, weak cup, scotch, bourbon, Dubonnet, cocktail?"

"Weak cup," I replied, after a moment's thought.

Phil said, "We won't give you much to eat because you're supposed to be having a real Christmas dinner with us later."

Someone had turned on some music. People were dancing clumsily in hunting boots in the library.

Mr. Miller slapped my back in passing. "Hallo, Jean. I hope the boys are looking after you all right," he said.

I drank some of the cup and screwed up my nose. "It's okay. It's quite weak," Phil said. The next moment he had strolled off to talk to a tall girl in hunting clothes.

"Let's go round the barn and look at the horses when you've finished your drink," Pete suggested. "I can't bear the din in here. That is if you don't want to dance," he added, on second thoughts.

"No fear," I replied.

We walked through the kitchen where there was an open fire burning. Annie was basting turkeys. I wished her a happy Christmas. Snow was falling fast and furiously outside.

"There'll be no more hunting while this lasts," Pete said.

"Well, you'll be in New York anyway," I replied,

imagining snow in the streets, on the roofs of trams, on hats and people's hair.

"Don't remind me," Pete said. "I hate that . . . city."

The horses were dozing in their boxes. When we came to Pete's chestnut, he said, "I've named her at last. I'm calling her Jean, after you."

I didn't know what to say, and for a moment I was stupidly embarrassed. Then I said. "You can't, it'll muddle everyone. Besides it's an awful name."

"What am I to call her then?" he asked. "You'll have to name her then."

"What about Firefly?" I suggested because it was the first name which came into my head.

"That'll do fine," he said.

We gave the horses sugar before we wandered indoors again. A great many guests had left in our absence.

"What have you been doing? Mooching, I suppose," Wendy said.

"Looking at the horses," I replied.

"We've named my mare Firefly," Pete told her.

Phil was dancing with the tall girl in the library. Angus was discussing English hunting with an elderly man in scarlet. Daddy was looking bored by the library fireplace. We could hear cars leaving.

"We'll soon be able to eat," Pete said.

"Why don't we take them upstairs and let them open their presents?" Wendy suggested. "I'm sure Angus is real tired of talking to that old five-star general."

"He likes the aged," I replied.

We waited until Angus had finished his conversation, before going upstairs together. Phil was still dancing in the library.

"We won't wait for him," Wendy said.

"We haven't opened ours from you. We thought it would be friendly to open them all together," Pete told us.

"Our others were all hung on the tree. Did you see it

in the library, all lit up? It's a real good tree," Wendy said.

Our presents were lying on Wendy's bed. Angus's and my wrapping looked bad and amateurish beside the Millers' efforts. It was annoying because we had taken particular trouble with the Millers' presents.

"I hope you like my present to you, Jean," Pete said.

"Gee, she ought to," Wendy exclaimed.

The first present opened was a joint one to Angus and me from Mr. and Mrs. Miller. Like the others, the wrapping-was sprayed with artificial snow and hung with decorative labels. Gold stars were stuck across the scarlet wrapping-paper. It was tied with gold binding. Inside we found two half-pint glass tankards with hunting scenes painted on them.

"They're for your mint juleps in the summer," Pete said. I wasn't sure what a mint julep was. "They're wonderful. What a lovely present," I said.

Pete had bought me a beautiful hunting-whip. It was something I had been wanting for ages, and I was terribly pleased. From Phil there was a book about a wild horse and from Wendy a silk scarf. Angus had a book on riding, and a head-collar from Phil and Wendy combined. The Millers were very pleased with their presents, and we all returned to the library feeling very gay.

Several people had been invited to dinner as well as ourselves. When the crowd was thinning, Wendy said, "Hi, Jean. Do you want to give Annie and me a hand with the serving up?"

Pete and Phil were collecting the dirty plates and glasses scattered about the house. I followed Wendy into the kitchen.

"We're having wild turkey. Daddy shot a few in the mountains some time back. They've been waiting in the deep freeze ever since," Wendy told me. Annie was dishing up asparagus. Wendy started to strain ears of corn. "You can light the candles, if you like," she said, handing me matches.

142

In the dining-room the table was laid. I lit the candles. There were fourteen places set ready. It was going to be a real dinner party. Mrs. Miller appeared in a low-cut velvet frock and ear-rings. She had put her hair up. "It's nice of you to help, Jean," she said.

She drew the curtains, hiding the snow still falling outside. "I hope it clears soon. I simply love New York," she told me.

Wendy entered bearing hot plates. "Everything's ready, Mummy. Shall I ring the bell?" she asked.

Ten minutes later there were fourteen of us sitting round the table. There was red wine in elegant glasses; and turkey and sweet potato, asparagus, corn. bread sauce, and hot rolls in front of each of us.

I was sitting between Phil and Pete; on Phil's left was the tall girl, who had changed into a coffee-coloured net frock. She seemed to be spending the night with the Millers. The vicar was eating heartily. He was fat and jovial and as he ate and drank his face grew steadily redder. Angus was between the tall girl and Wendy. No one proposed any toasts; everyone talked a great deal. At one moment we were all being Scottish and throwing salt over our left shoulders and drinking to the queen across the water. The tall girl spoke with a real Southern drawl. She must have been about eighteen. Peach Melba followed the turkey. Pete, Angus and Phil cleared away the plates and fetched more wine from the bar. Dinner seemed to go on and on. At last we reached the coffee stage. The vicar's face was the colour of beetroot by now; I was glad I hadn't come in hunting-clothes, because suddenly the room seemed very hot. I was beginning to feel sleepy. I could see Angus gazing at me anxiously. He was afraid I would fall asleep and disgrace us all.

Phil talked endlessly to the tall girl, who seemed to be called Pauline. Pete had nothing left to say. Nearly everyone else was laughing and telling funny stories.

When we had finished our coffee, Pete said, "Come on, let's go."

"What about the clearing up?" I asked.

"We can do that in the morning," he replied.

We went upstairs to Wendy's room and Pete switched on the television. Presently, Wendy and Angus joined us. I think we watched some sort of revue. I can't remember much, because I kept falling asleep. Occasionally Pete said, "Are you sure you wouldn't rather do something else?" and we all said "No" firmly.

Angus said, "Do try and stay awake, Jean," and I knew he thought I was being rude, but I couldn't do anything about it, my eyelids were heavy with sleep. Pete changed the programme and said, "Do you find this more interesting?" and I saw doctors visiting hospitals on the screen and screamed, "No, it reminds me of Angus falling off in the mountains."

Some time much later Daddy appeared and said, "Come on, we must go home. It's long past midnight."

Pete fetched my coat and we thanked each other all over again for everything. There was nearly a foot of snow when we stepped outside and it was still falling. The car was waiting for us by the front door. We said good-bye and thank you and then we drove away through the snow. "We'll need chains if this lasts," Daddy said.

"Well, did you enjoy yourselves?" Mummy asked.

"It was okay. I liked the turkey," my brother answered. It seemed ages since we had left home. "It went on too long," I said. It was very light in the valley. I looked across to the mountains capped with snow. I thought of the wild horse roaming alone in a white world.

"Phil and Pete want me to go shooting with them to-morrow. They don't go to New York until the evening," Angus said.

"Oh lord," exclaimed Mummy. "Do you think you're safe?"

"I've been shooting before," Angus replied.

"If only you'll be sensible," Mummy said.

The mountains looked cold and remorseless beneath the snow. I wondered what the wild horse would find to eat in his cold white world. He might be starving, I thought, gazing beyond the mountains to the cold grey sky.

"Everyone goes shooting, only they call it hunting, on Boxing Day. All the men, anyway," Angus said.

"I can't see why you want to be like everyone else," Daddy replied.

He may be hung up by his head-collar. or trapped in a ravine, I decided, and suddenly I knew that, come what may, on the morrow I would search again for the wild horse.

"All right, you can go. But don't be foolish," Daddy said. "Remember that a gun is a lethal weapon."

We had to fetch spades and shovel the snow away from the garage before we could put the car inside. The air was damp and cold. The kitchen was cold. The bay mare whinnied and Angus and I mixed her another feed. She was shivering under her rug, so I fetched a blanket off my bed and put that on too. She seemed warmer then, and we stood and rubbed her ears and talked until Daddy called from the house.

Mummy had made tea. We sat about the kitchen and discussed the evening. I didn't say much. I had started to think about the wild horse again, and to make plans. Something told me that he needed help and there seemed nothing to stop me looking for him on Boxing Day in the mountains. I saw myself riding endlessly through snow. I shall have to avoid the guns, I thought, I don't want to die yet.

I dreamed all night about the wild horse: I was driving him down mountain passes blocked with snow and ice; I was schooling in the paddock at home in England; I was jumping him at Wembley. I wakened to a white world and a cold pale sun. The sky was blue. The snow had stopped falling.

CHAPTER FOURTEEN

I KNEW at once that it was Boxing Day. I rushed to the window and saw that the snow outside was crisp and knew that there had been frost. I dressed quickly in my sky-blue jersey and jodhpurs. Outside the air was sharp; the snow crunched under my feet. The bay mare heard the back door slam and whinnied. I felt as though I was setting out on a tremendous expedition, as I mixed her feed. I might have been about to climb Everest. It was that sort of morning.

I sang as I boiled a kettle in the kitchen. I rushed upstairs with tea for everyone.

"You're shooting to-day," I told Angus, because he can't remember things early in the morning, and I knew he would be furious if he slept till ten o'clock by mistake.

Daddy said, "Why so early?"

I couldn't stop to explain. I felt in a tremendous hurry. I wanted to be riding alone in the mountains seeking the wild horse. "It's a quarter past eight," I answered, as I left the room and rushed downstairs.

I mucked out the bay mare's box in ten minutes. Then I started to make toast for breakfast.

"What's the hurry?" Angus asked, appearing yawning in the kitchen. "It's not you who's shooting."

"I know. But I'm going to find the wild horse," I answered. "He may be starving."

"What, in this weather? Do you think you'll be allowed to go?" Angus asked. He sounded as though he didn't think it likely.

"I'm going, whatever anybody says. We can't leave him to starve. It's cruelty to animals," I replied.

"Be careful we don't shoot you. Anyway, I don't believe he's around here at all. Everybody thinks he's moved on," Angus said.

"Well, I'm just going to make sure," I replied. "And now look what you've made me do," I cried, as the kettle boiled all over the stove.

"It's nothing to do with me. You've simply filled it too full," Angus said.

I felt all on edge, and now I was terrified that my parents would forbid an expedition into the mountains.

"Why don't you come shooting? Wendy is," Angus said.

"No, thank you. I don't feel like killing things," I replied. "Do you think Mummy and Daddy are ever coming down? Do you think we can start without them?" I asked.

"Why don't you get breakfast and then get going before anyone comes down to say no? That's what I would do," Angus said.

I knew that it was a bad suggestion. But I couldn't bear the thought of not going. "Won't you get the blame then? I don't want you to be stopped shooting," I answered, making coffee.

"That doesn't matter. It's your expedition which matters," my brother said. "Here, you go," he added, seizing a jug out of my hand. "I'll make the coffee." I said, "Thanks, terribly," and I snatched a hunk of bread and spread it with butter, and rushed out to the stable munching. I filled my pockets with oats and fetched a halter and the bay mare's tack.

Two minutes later I was mounting in the yard. "Good luck," Angus called softly from the back door. I shouted, "Thank you," and "Good-bye," but he had already returned to the kitchen. I hoped he wouldn't get into trouble as I rode out of the yard into the white world.

The snow was just crisp enough to avoid balling. The bay mare was fresh and wouldn't walk. I trotted briskly across the sparkling snow, feeling as though I belonged to the distant past, before the advent of cars and the machine age.

The Hereford cattle were clustered around the Millers'

147

farm waiting to be fed. Ground hogs and deer had left prints in the snow. The valley seemed empty and quite devoid of sound. It wasn't the valley I knew any more— just a vast white wilderness.

The trail leading into the mountains looked smaller and quite different beneath the snow. The coated trees had thawed a little before they froze, so that now weird, fantastic icicles encased their branches like thick glass. The bay mare's hoofs made fresh prints in the snow and it was obvious she and I were the first beings to tread the trail since Christmas night. There was the tiniest breeze which faintly stirred the encrusted leaves and made the trees creak uneasily; otherwise there was no sound and we might have been travelling through a dead world.

I thought of my parents eating breakfast at home; cracking the tops of boiled eggs, spreading toast with butter and marmalade. I hoped they weren't too angry at my behaviour; for though I was certain that I was on an errand of mercy, I was afraid they wouldn't see my expedition in the same light.

It was hard work following the trail; soon the bay mare was sweating and I was watching her ears to avoid the glare from the snow. I came to a fork and turned left for no particular reason. Here deer had left tracks in the virgin snow. My hands were cold in my gay, new gloves and my feet were cold inside my shoes. The sky had turned a miraculous blue, the sort of blue which belongs to the Riviera and the South of France. The sun was melting the snow where it reached the tree tops. It was the sort of day and setting one dreams about.

I don't know how long I rode nor how far before I saw the first hoofprints in the snow, and knew that my hunch was right and that somewhere not far away the wild horse walked alone through the mountains. I began to feel excited then, because I knew that my journey was justified and that there was hope again on the horizon. I hurried the bay mare and I think she knew that we were near our goal, for she seemed to take new heart.

Soon I heard the distant sound of firing and, in my imagination, I saw the Millers and Angus ploughing through the snow with guns. Then the hoofprints left the trail and we were plodding through undergrowth and under trees and over half-buried rocks. I think the bay mare could smell the Palomino, for she seemed to follow the hoofprints with great eagerness and once or twice she stopped to smell the air.

I started to wonder what would happen when the wild horse saw us. I dreaded an exciting chase. Where the snow was melting beneath the sun it formed into hard balls in the bay mare's hoofs and several times she stumbled and almost fell. Once she seemed to be walking on stilts, and I was about to dismount when the ball fell out and lay a dirty grey lump on the white snow.

I had been lost for some time when we reached a tiny clearing and saw, standing alone beneath a tree, a horse coated with snow and ice. It was the Palomino, but he looked quite different. He seemed half asleep and icicles hung from his mane and fetlocks; his ribs showed through the snow on his sides; and his eyes were partly closed and dull as though life didn't interest him any more. In spite of his awful appearance, my heart gave a leap of joy, for at last I had found him, at least he was still alive.

He raised his head a little as we approached, and the bay mare whinnied softly. A tattered head-collar hung on his tired head. I'd never seen a horse look so weary before. I was nearly crying as I dismounted from the bay mare. I felt no triumph at all.

I said, "Hallo, whoa little horse," as I approached the Palomino, and though his tired eyes watched me warily, he didn't move. I knew then that he was very sick. I reached out a hand and took the piece of rope which dangled from his head-collar and still he didn't move. I saw that his eyes were almost yellow and so were his nostrils and his mouth. I wondered then whether he was strong enough to journey home. I tied the halter I had brought on to his head-collar and brushed the snow off his thin, drooping neck. The bay mare rubbed her head against him, but he gave no response.

He wouldn't eat the oats out of my pockets. I rubbed his cold, half-frozen ears and I could feel him falling to sleep again. I knew then that somehow I had to get him home and that he would never stand another night in the mountains. I guessed that he had come to the clearing

A horse coated with snow and ice

in the small hours and that he hadn't moved since; it looked as though it had been his home for some time.

I stood and wished that I had Angus with me and that I was in England and could reach a telephone in a few minutes and summon a horse-box. I wished that Pete was with me because I was sure he would know how to handle the situation. I felt very helpless alone in the mountains with the two horses. My hands were numb and snow from the few thawing trees had dripped down by neck. At that moment I hated Virginia and the Blue Ridge Mountains more than anywhere else in the world. I hated the icicles and the snow and the endless trails which all looked just alike. I hated the sky and the sun and the remoteness and the few birds now hovering in the air looking for dying animals to eat.

Wendy had told me once about these birds. She called them an omen of death; and now they were just above, cawing greedily—a hungry flock of birds waiting for the Palomino to die.

I knew I couldn't leave the Palomino to seek help when I saw the birds. I was frightened that they would swoop while I was away and when I returned I would find only a heap of newly picked bones. I had heard that these birds didn't wait for animals to die, only until they were too weak to fight any more, then they descended and the mountains echoed with the screams of the dying animal.

The birds made up my mind for me. I pulled gently on the halter and said, "Come on, phantom horse, we're going home." He looked like a phantom covered with snow—a phantom ghost on his last pilgrimage.

The bay mare encouraged him with another whinny. I think she knew how ill he was. At last my words and the pull on his head-collar seemed to reach his brain; he moved with awkward stiff steps as though his limbs were frozen. He was so pitiful that I cried and my tears made little holes in the snow. I had to go back the way I had come because it was the only way I knew.

I followed the bay mare's hoofprints back through the undergrowth, under the trees and over the rocks. Every few minutes I had to stop and let the Palomino rest. It was ages before I reached the trail again.

And then I saw that the weather had changed. The sun had gone. The sky was no longer blue, but the sort of grey which means snow. The air was much warmer;

and I knew that I had to hurry because soon there would
be fresh snow which would obliterate the hoofprints and
then I would be really lost. Already the snow was soft
on the trail. I sunk in a foot each time I took a step and
my jodhpurs were soon soaking right up to the knee.
I walked between the two horses and the bay mare hurried
and the Palomino lagged; it wasn't a pleasant journey.

And then the snow came in large, white flakes. It fell
on my hair, on the horses, on the trail and the trees and
undergrowth, it fell as though it would never stop falling.

I thought of the time then, of my parents waiting
anxiously at home. I began to wonder whether I should
ever reach the warmth and safety of Mountain Farm
while it was still possible. Nobody was shooting any
more. The mountains were wrapped in silence except
for the shifty, eerie sound of falling snow; all prints had
vanished, nothing seemed to live except myself and the
two horses.

I started to wish that I had brought provisions. My
tummy told me that it was lunch time; my legs felt
weak and I longed for a bar of chocolate or a large ham
sandwich. I tried to heighten my morale by imagining
the Palomino in the stable at home, but when I looked
at him and saw his utter weariness I started to wonder
whether he would live if we ever did reach home.

I shall never forget the next few hours. We plodded
on and on and the trail looked just the same. And the
bay mare started to tire and to look back as though we
had taken the wrong turning and were now walking
directly away from home. And I began to worry, I saw
night falling. the snow deepening. I wondered whether
my parents would send out a search party. I felt terribly
guilty, and for a moment I wished I hadn't listened to
Angus's advice in the morning; then I looked at the
Palomino again and suddenly I didn't regret anything
any more. It was so wonderful to think that if he lived
he would really be ours.

I thought of hunting him across a russet and gold Virginian countryside, of seeing him from my window early in the morning and knowing that he was ours, of feeding him late at night and riding him in the spring. I saw us jumping in shows, competing in hunter trials, bringing home the tri-coloured rosette. I saw myself rounding up cattle on him with Phil and Pete, schooling him in the paddock at home, I saw him wearing elegant rugs with our initials in one corner. I plodded on through the snow lost in my own happy imagination, ceasing to notice my aching legs, the feeling of afternoon, or the falling, endless snow.

Dusk came quite suddenly, it came with a darkening sky and a whispering evening breeze. I had followed the same trail for hours, yet nothing seemed changed. Both horses were dragging by this time, and I'm sure they knew I was lost. When I halted, the Palomino stood drearily with hanging head, and a sickly eye which showed no interest at all in anything. I looked down the trail and, reasoning that we must reach somewhere some time, I plodded on. The wind blew the snow in our faces and my eyes started to run, and my gloves were wet from where the snow had melted when it met the warmth of my hands. I started to sing to raise my spirits. I sang songs from American musicals and "Tipperary." Then I began singing hymns.

Because of the snow, night came without darkness. And then, quite suddenly, I saw twinkling lights shining through the trees. I started to hurry then and I shouted to the horses, "Come on. We're getting somewhere at last." But they wouldn't hurry; they had lost all confidence in me; they dragged and the snow balled more and more in their hoofs, and they stumbled and jerked my arms, while I pulled frantically on the rope and the reins, losing all sense and reason in a wild desire to reach the twinkling lights.

Then I thought of shouting. "I'm coming. Is there anyone about? I've caught the wild horse," I called and my voice echoed and came back muffled by the sound of falling snow.

I hurried on and gradually the lights seemed nearer. The snow was very deep now and soft and wet, so that it was hard work moving at all.

An then I thought I heard an answering call, and I started to shout twice as loud. "It's Jean. I'm all right. I've got the wild horse," I yelled over and over again.

Soon I could feel a stronger breeze blowing through the trees and, quite suddenly, there was more light and space, and we had reached a valley, and, with a cry of joy, I saw that it was our valley.

I tried to run and fell sprawling in the snow. The horses waited patiently until I was on my feet again; and the bay mare raised her head and looked across the valley to where the lights shone bravely in Mountain Farm.

I remember hoping that there would be someone at home when I arrived. I was terrified lest the whole district should be out searching for me. And now I saw that there were lots of little lights moving about the valley. There were tiresome little gusts of snow, and drifts. I started to shout, "I'm coming, I'm coming, I'm coming," until the words were all jumbled together and didn't make sense any more.

The bay mare was hurrying too now. She jogged and bumped the Palomino and he stumbled and almost fell. I slackened my pace then. I didn't want to take a dead horse home.

I talked to the Palomino. "Soon you'll be in a lovely warm stable, a really super one." I told him. "There'll be lots to eat and gradually you'll get well again."

I stopped and patted him and rubbed his ears and he stood with his legs sprawled apart as though he couldn't move another step. If it had been possible to get a horse-box to him I think I would have left him there, but as it was I had to keep him moving.

Then I thought I heard a shout and I started to call

again and someone called, "It's Jean. She's reached the valley." After that there was a great deal of shouting and suddenly a bell rang out loud and clear, drowning the voices and the sound of falling snow. Lights seemed to be moving towards me from all directions and the bay mare was dragging me faster and faster towards Mountain Farm, and, somewhere behind me, the Palomino was dragging on my other arm until I thought it must fall from its socket. And I kept yelling, "It's Jean. I'm home," till someone said quite close, "It's all right now, we know," and I saw my brother and beyond him the back door standing open.

"I've got the wild horse," I said. "But he's terribly ill. I think we should have the vet at once. He's almost dead. That's why I've been so long." I started to cry then, because the Palomino really did look ill, and I was suddenly sure that he wouldn't last more than a few hours, because his eyes looked sunken in their sockets and he was hardly breathing any more.

"Let's get him inside," Angus said.

"Where are Mummy and Daddy?" I asked.

"Looking for you," Angus replied, taking the bay mare. "It's all right. They will have heard the bell; that was to be the signal."

"You mean that I was home?" I asked, and Angus nodded.

The Palomino tottered into the empty loose-box. He seemed in a coma. I don't think he had any idea where he was.

I shut the box door. "I'll ring up the vet," I said. I felt I must do it immediately, before my parents arrived and I had to explain.

I asked the exchange to put me through to the nearest vet, and the girl who answered said, "Will Doctor Beecher do?"

I almost replied, "No, I want a vet not a doctor," before I remembered that vets are called doctors in America. "Sure. Fine," I answered.

155

"*I've got the wild horse*"

I saw that the snow on my clothes was melting in pools on the hall floor. Then Dr. Beecher answered and I told him what had happened, speaking as slowly and coherently as I could. When I had finished speaking, he said, "Okay, I'll be right over," and hung up. I thought of him hurrying for his coat, starting his car. Then I began to wonder whether he would ever reach us on such a night.

Angus had settled the bay mare when I returned to the stable. She had piles of straw under her rugs and was munching a hot feed.

"I had it all ready," he said. "But I don't know what to do about the Palomino. He won't eat a thing."

"He's awfully ill. Have you noticed how yellow he is?" I asked.

"Let's hope the vet can do something," my brother replied.

"Hallo, are you there, Jean?" someone called, and I saw my parents wading through the snow.

"Yes, I'm back. I've got the wild horse. He's terribly ill. I think he's dying. That's why I've been so long."

I was afraid they would be angry. But Daddy said, "We thought it was something like that."

And Mummy said, "If only you would choose better weather for your expeditions. But perhaps now you've got the wretched horse, you'll stop giving us frights."

"I'm terribly sorry. I didn't mean to stay out so long." I replied.

"It doesn't matter," Mummy answered.

There were more voices now and Pete and Phil and Wendy came into the yard.

"Congratulations, Jean," Pete said, taking my hand.

"He's terribly ill," I replied quickly. "He may die." I didn't want congratulations. I didn't think bringing a sick horse home was a deed which deserved congratulations—it's something you do expecting no reward, I thought, besides, no one with a heart could have left the Palomino to die in the mountains.

157

"I've rung up the vet. He's coming right over," I said.

"You'd better come in and change. You look soaked," Mummy said.

"What about the Palomino? He shouldn't be le alone," I cried.

"We'll look after him," Daddy answered. "Hurry u and have a hot bath and get some food inside you. The we can talk."

I went indoors with Mummy and she pulled off my we jodhpurs and I suddenly discovered that I was terribl tired and ravenously hungry.

I ate some bread and butter and had a hot bath an changed. There was hot soup waiting for me in the kitchen and braised ham and potatoes.

Angus was leaning against the stove. "The vet hasn't come yet. I've sent the Millers home," he told me. "Wendy would talk and the Palomino needs quiet."

"I thought they were going to New York," I replied.

"The weather's stopped them. The road's blocked near Baltimore," Angus said.

"Did you have a good shoot?" I asked, remembering the morning, which seemed so long ago.

"No, the snow was too deep. We hardly killed anything. By the way, I told Mummy and Daddy that you probably wouldn't be back to lunch. That's why they didn't start worrying till tea time."

I looked at the clock and saw that it was six o'clock. I had imagined that it was nearly supper time.

"Were they furious?" I asked.

"They were rather," Angus answered. "They said that you were going potty over the wild horse."

Mummy and Daddy came in from the stables.

"He does look in a bad way. I think I'll ring up Smythe. He'd better know we've got his horse," Daddy told us.

"Jean's horse now," Angus replied.

"Yours too. Because if it hadn't been for you I wouldn't have gone," I told Angus.

It was ages before Dr. Beecher came. We had all eaten

supper by that time, taking it in turns to watch the Palomino. Daddy had talked to Mr. Smythe for hours on the telephone, and we knew now that if the Palomino lived he would be ours for ever and ever.

At last, there was a knock on the back door and a small man stood in the yard clutching a black bag.

"I'm real sorry I've been so long. I've walked the last three miles, the road's blocked by a ten-foot wall of snow," he said.

I liked Dr. Beecher at once. We all hurried to the stable where Angus was watching the Palomino. The vet didn't talk much.

He murmured. "Gee, he's bad. He's eaten something really bad." Then he mentioned poison and jaundice and found the Palomino had a temperature of a hundred and five. He gave him three injections and stood and looked at him for some time.

"There's nothing more we can do to-night but hope," he said at last. "I'll stop by first thing to-morrow."

"Are you sure you wouldn't like to stay the night?" Mummy asked.

"Thank you, Ma'am. I guess I'd better not. Maybe I'll get some more calls to-night," Dr. Beecher replied.

It was very quiet when Dr. Beecher had left.

"Well, that's that. We can do no more," Daddy said.

"What were the injections?" Angus asked.

"Penicillin, iron and liver—or some sort of food or vitamins—I don't know what the other one was," Daddy replied.

"He's bringing some sort of drench in the morning," Mummy said.

We looked at the Palomino before we went to bed. He was lying down and he looked happier, though still terribly ill.

"Do you think he will live?" I asked Daddy.

"Who can tell? We can only hope, as Dr. Beecher said," Daddy replied.

I hated going to bed. Outside the snow was still falling.

It seemed sad to have caught the wild horse at last and not to know whether he would live or die. Nor that I cared very much whose horse he was—I only wanted him to live.

I prayed for the Palomino before I fell asleep. I remember Angus coming into my room and saying: "If he lives, let's call him Phantom, because he looked like a phantom coming across the valley with you to-night, all covered with snow and thin and out of another world."

"All right," I answered. "If he lives."

And now everything is nearly told. For the Palomino lived; after three days of hovering between life and death, he stood on his legs again and looked over his loose-box door.

As Angus suggested, we named him Phantom, and, perhaps because of our English accents or perhaps because we rescued him, he seems to love Mountain Farm and whinnies when he sees us, and is much loved by us all.

Since Phantom came to live with us, Angus and I have become much nicer and far more sensible. We don't get lost any more because he always knows the way home; and we don't lose our heads, because now he's ours, there doesn't seem anything worth pursuing through the ever-changing Blue Ridge Mountains of Virginia.